This Book Belongs To:

CONTENTS

WRITTEN AND EDITED BY JAMES HENDERSON
ILLUSTRATED BY JOHN HARROLD
STORY COLOURING BY DORIS CAMPBELL

ISBN 0-85079-168-5

RUPERT

John Harrold.

£3·25

RUPERT and

All four pals meant to start today
Their boat and camping holiday.

For weeks Rupert and Bingo with Algy Pug and Bill Badger have been planning a river camping holiday. They will explore the river by boat during the day and camp beside it each night. But they are just about to leave when Bill and Algy find a fault in their boat which must be put right. "We'll go ahead," Rupert says. "We shall camp tonight and wait for you to catch up tomorrow."

the RIVER PIRATES

But Bill and Algy must delay
Their setting out until next day.

"That sun glint up there on the slope!
It's someone with a telescope."

So off row Rupert and Bingo, taking it easy for they don't want to get too far ahead. They have been going for only a little when Rupert spots something! "That flashing on the hill!" he says. "The sun is glinting on a telescope. Someone's watching us." Nearer they see that the watcher is a man. Then they see him close his telescope and signal to someone with a scarf or neckerchief.

Now they can see him signalling
With his 'kerchief or some such thing.

RUPERT'S BOAT ACTS STRANGELY

The river that's been smooth 'til now
Begins to swirl about their bow.

The boat is dragged, against their will,
Into the bank below the hill.

"We're going to hit!" the two pals wail.
Then in a tunnel thing they sail.

Now Rupert grabs a branch but – crack!
It snaps and he sprawls on his back.

"That's odd," Bingo muses. "Someone examines us through a telescope then starts signalling. Do you think it was about us?" But Rupert doesn't answer. He has noticed something just as strange – and more frightening. The water, smooth until now, is swirling round the boat in an alarming way. He digs the paddle in hard and tries to steer. "It's no use, Bingo!" he gasps. "I can't control the boat. We're being pulled into the bank!" Bingo gives a gasp of horror as the dense bushes and trees on the bank loom closer and closer. Rupert keeps trying to turn the boat. It is hopeless. Then when it seems they are going to crash the bushes part and they see they are being drawn into a low tunnel. Rupert drops the paddle, springs onto his seat and grabs an overhanging branch. For a moment the boat slows. Then . . . crr-a-ack . . . the branch snaps and Rupert goes sprawling in the boat.

RUPERT GOES THROUGH A TUNNEL

Rupert and Bingo hold on tight.
Ahead now they can see daylight.

Out of the tunnel worse awaits –
They're racing hard towards sluice gates!

"We're going to crash!" poor Bingo squeals.
Next moment they're head over heels!

They haven't crashed. Their bow has met,
With such a jolt, a winched-up net.

The rushing water booms inside the tunnel as Rupert and Bingo are swept along. Ahead they see a glimmer of light which grows fast as they race towards it. Then suddenly they are in daylight in a narrow channel with steep stone sides. But their feeling of relief lasts only a moment for they are still travelling at great speed. And just ahead of them is a very solid-looking sluice gate. Horrified, they watch it loom larger and larger. Then as it seems the boat must smash into the gate it stops with a jolt pitching the pals head over heels. The nose of the boat is pressed against a stout net which has sprung out of the water. "What on earth . . .?" Bingo gasps as he picks himself up. Rupert says nothing. He is staring at a figure on the bank. It is a very old pirate, brandishing a rusty cutlass. On the other side a second old pirate is securing the rope which pulled up the net.

RUPERT IS CAUGHT BY PIRATES

The shaken chums have, it appears,
Been trapped by ancient buccaneers.

Our two are hustled through a door,
Wondering what may lie in store.

The man named Ben says, "Here you'll stay
Until your parents ransom pay."

And now there comes into the mill
The one who signalled from the hill.

"Pull 'em in, Josh!" cries the old pirate as he totters across the top of the sluice gate. "Ay, ay, Ben," quavers the other and drags the pals' craft to the bank with a boathook. "Out ye get!" he cries. Rupert and Bingo scramble from the boat. They are speechless. Everything has happened so fast. "Into the mill!" pipes Ben and points with his sword at the building behind him. It is a deserted-looking place with a tunnel in the middle through which water races. The inside echoes with the sound of the water. "Oh, please," Rupert begs, "What do you want with us?" Ben who seems to be in charge points a shaky finger and croaks, "What we want is ransom! Ye're our prisoners and here you'll stay 'til your families pay ransom for ye." Just then the door opens and in comes yet another very old pirate. He is knotting a 'kerchief about his neck. "I'm sure he's the one we saw signalling," Bingo whispers.

RUPERT HEARS THE PIRATE PLAN

Ben tells him, "Tom, go up the stair
And in the big loft lock this pair."

"Too aged for the Spanish Main,"
Says Tom, "we three came home again."

"That tunnel ought to have a grille
So's boats don't get dragged to the mill."

"But we three took the grille away
As you two youngsters found today!"

"Young Tom, take the prisoners to the loft and lock 'em in," Ben orders the newcomer. Young Tom, who looks just as old as the others, ushers Rupert and Bingo up to a loft stretching the length of the mill. Even here the rumbling of the water is loud. "Do this, do that," grumbles Tom. "Like I was still a cabin boy. That Ben forgets 'twas my idea to use the old mill to trap boats. 'Tain't fair." "No it isn't," chorus Bingo and Rupert who want to keep Tom talking. Delighted to have someone listen to him for a change, Tom tells the pals how he and the others decided to become river pirates when they got too old for pirating on the Spanish Main. He remembered the old mill and how its wheel was driven by water drawn from the river through a culvert when the sluice was opened wide. There was a grille or grating on it to stop boats being drawn in. "So I told 'em, remove the grating and we can pull in boats – and ransom prisoners," Tom gloats.

RUPERT FINDS A TRAPDOOR

"Rupert, somehow we must get free
And tell the police about those three."

To find a way the two explore,
And Rupert spots an old trapdoor.

"It's where the mill-wheel used to be.
But wait! The water's slowing. See?"

They're winding shut, those aged two,
The sluice that lets the water through.

"Young Tom, stop wasting time up there," Ben calls from below. Tom pulls a face but he still scurries off, locking the door. "Rupert, now that we know what they're up to we must escape and tell the police," Bingo says. "Let's see if there's anything up here we can use." So the pals start poking about among old bits of mill equipment. Suddenly Rupert calls, "Look!" Bingo looks up from the things he has found to see his pal holding open an old trapdoor. Next moment the two are peering at the mill-stream racing through the tunnel. "It's where the mill-wheel was," Bingo breathes. "You can see the axle stumps . . . but wait! The water's slowing. They must be shutting the sluice." Rupert scambles across to a window and looks out. Sure enough, Josh and Young Tom are winding shut the underwater "doors" that let the stream through the gate. And Tom is still complaining about being ordered around.

RUPERT SIGNS A RANSOM NOTE

*"It's now so quiet we're sure to know
When those three let the water flow."*

*Cries Bingo, "Here's some useful gear."
"Hush!" Rupert says. "They're coming here."*

*"You'll write your parents and you'll say
To get you back they'll have to pay."*

*And Ben goes on, "If you don't write
You'll have no supper here tonight."*

When the pals lower the trapdoor they notice something – how quiet it is now that the water is not running. "We'll be able to tell any time they open the sluice," Bingo says. Before Rupert can ask why that's important Bingo goes on, "I have an idea for escaping. Some of this old stuff in here will be useful. You keep watch while I sort it out." A little later Bingo has to drag a tarpaulin over his bits and pieces when Rupert hisses, "They're coming up here!"

The door opens and in file the pirates. Ben is carrying paper and a quill pen. The pals, he announces, must write to their parents to say they won't be set free until ransom is paid. He tries to look fierce and says, "If ye don't ye shall have no supper!" "Ay, and we 'as good ones," pipes Josh. "Chips and jam sangwidges." Since they are planning to escape, anyway, the pals sign. What's more, they're very hungry . . . even for jam sandwiches with chips.

RUPERT'S PAL PLANS A RAFT

"The first of many ransom notes!
Now we'll start pulling in more boats."

"Now," Bingo says, "here's what we'll do
Next time they let the water through."

"We'll make a raft, that is my scheme,
And lower it to the running stream."

They just have time to hide their gear
Before two of the men appear.

"They're awful pirates," Rupert thinks. "They haven't said how much ransom they want nor even got our addresses." But the old pirates seem happy enough. "The first o' many ransom notes!" Ben crows. "We'll be pulling boats in all the time now!" "That's what I wanted to know," says Bingo when the pirates have gone. "They'll have to open the sluice. That's what we need." And he whips the cover off the pile of old mill equipment he has found. His main find is a pallet that was used for lowering sacks of flour in the old days. With it are several oil cans, rope, twine and a pulley. Rupert sees at once what Bingo plans – a raft! "Right!" Bingo says. "We'll start it after supper when the pirates have gone to bed." As it is, they just have time to hide the things before supper arrives. "We brought you a lamp," Josh says. "In case you don't like the dark." Plainly, he is trying hard not to sound kindly.

RUPERT HELPS WITH THE RAFT

When supper's done the pals set to.
There's such a lot they have to do.

At last it's done. They've made the raft,
A makeshift but a sturdy craft.

Now there remains just one thing more,
The means to lower it through the floor.

And now the pair are set to go
When they can hear the stream below.

Grateful for the light Josh brought, our two start work when supper has been cleared away. Using Bingo's pocket-knife they cut lengths of twine to tie oil cans to the pallet. "This will help to keep the raft afloat," Bingo whispers. Long past their usual bedtime the pals work on their raft. At last it is done. "That should do," Bingo says. "I think it's strong enough." "How do we get it into the water?" Rupert asks. "I've worked that out," says Bingo. "We lower it, as it used to be lowered with sacks of flour – except that we drop it through the trapdoor into the water when it's moving fast." So while Rupert ties lines to the rings on the pallet Bingo gets the pulley rigged. At last all is ready. They pull the tarpaulin over their craft and climb onto their mattresses. "We must be ready to go the first time they open the sluice gate and the water starts running again," Bingo says. "Goodnight, Rupert."

RUPERT SPIES ON THE PIRATES

The pals awake at break of day.
The men bring in their breakfast tray.

Young Tom's inclined to stay and chat,
But Ben says there's no time for that.

And off the pals soon see Tom trot
Towards his hilltop lookout spot.

"Tom's signalling to them below,"
Says Rupert. "Let's get set to go."

"Rise and shine!" Rupert and Bingo stir at the call to find a sunny morning and that the three old pirates have brought their breakfast – tea and bread spread with condensed milk. The pirates don't even glance at where the raft is hidden. Instead they watch the pals breakfast as if anxious they should enjoy it. Suddenly Ben turns on Tom: "Time's wasting. Off to your lookout post and watch for boats." The pals exchange a "get ready" look.

The pals listen to the pirates clattering downstairs then they go to the window. In a moment they see the pirates emerge from the mill. Ben and Josh settle themselves on a bench. Tom sets off for the hilltop, muttering to himself. For a long time nothing happens as Tom sweeps the river with his telescope. Suddenly Rupert calls urgently to Bingo who is checking the raft, "He's waving his scarf. He must have spotted a boat."

RUPERT GETS READY TO ESCAPE

The old men open up the gate
That sets the mill-stream in full spate.

The pals act fast. They rig the rope.
This is their chance to flee, they hope.

Now open up the old trapdoor.
My goodness, hear that water roar!

They're nervous but they cannot stay.
"Right," Rupert says. "Let's lower away."

As soon as Ben and Josh spot Tom's signal they totter to the sluice gate and start to wind it open. The pals spring into action. A rope fixed to the raft is fed through the pulley. Bingo climbs onto a box to hang the pulley from a hook over the trapdoor. Rupert leads the lowering rope through a ring on the floor. Everything is as ready as it can be. Above the clanking of the sluice being opened the pals hear water beginning to race through the tunnel.

They open the trapdoor. Now neither feels quite so brave. They gasp at the sight of the mill-stream racing and roaring beneath them. Can their makeshift craft really stand up to that sort of thing? Well, there's one way to find out. "Come on," says Bingo. "No point in waiting. Let's get it into the water." They let go the lowering line from its ring and take the weight of their raft. They ease it towards the opening. "Right, lower away!" Rupert says.

15

RUPERT HAS TO JUMP FOR IT

Just see that poor raft lurch and sway.
Brave Bingo says he'll lead the way.

It's Rupert's turn. He doesn't wait.
This is no time to hesitate.

He drops. He hangs on for dear life.
Now Bingo has got out his knife.

He saws the rope. It strains. It parts.
And down the stream the pals' raft darts.

Feeding out the line a little at a time, Rupert and Bingo at last have the raft on the water. "My plan, so I'll go first," Bingo says. Rupert secures the lowering line and Bingo climbs down it to the raft. He makes it! Now it is Rupert's turn. The rope he must climb down is jerking and bucking as the mill-stream tries to carry the raft away. Nothing for it! He takes a deep breath and launches himself at the wildly bucking rope.

Rupert manages to grab the rope but it is jerking so wildly that in order not to be smashed against the sides of the tunnel he has to let go. Down he plunges towards the racing mill-stream. Bingo grabs him as he drops and drags him onto the raft. "Hold tight!" he shouts and slashes at the rope with his knife. It parts. The raft leaps free and he sprawls beside Rupert, hanging on desperately as the raft goes bucketing along.

Rupert and the River Pirates

RUPERT RIDES THE MILL-STREAM

"I say," gasps Rupert, "what a ride!"
Let's hope that we don't hit the side."

Then some way up ahead he sees
The mill-stream races into trees.

Below the trees it's gloomy green.
But wait! Now sunlight's to be seen.

"Well!" Bingo cries. "For goodness' sake!
I know this place – Nutchester Lake!"

The roaring mill-stream is so loud that the pals can't hear if the pirates have noticed their escape. Anyway, they're too busy hanging onto the raft. 'Where do you think this goes?" Rupert gasps. "No idea!" Bingo shouts. "Let's hope we don't hit the sides and get wrecked." Rupert who hasn't thought of this, gulps. Then they see ahead of them that the mill-stream disappears into a screen of trees. "Now what?" Rupert wonders.

Just then Bingo cries, "Look out! Branches!" He throws himself flat. So does Rupert, just in time to escape being swept from the raft by a low-hanging branch. The trees are so dense and close that sunlight can't get through and the pals are carried along in a greeny gloom. Not knowing what lies ahead is frightening. Then it begins to get lighter. The sunlight gets stronger and from somewhere ahead Rupert and Bingo hear a loud buzzing noise.

RUPERT IS RESCUED

A motor boat hoves into sight.
They hope the owner spots their plight.

He does, and takes the raft in tow.
"Now, what's all this?" he wants to know.

He hears their tale then says, "Let's go
And tell the police. They ought to know."

"Can I believe this tale, you two?
I think I'll ring and check on you."

"Nutchester Lake!" exclaims Bingo. And there ahead is the source of the buzzing sound – a motorboat! "Ahoy!" the pals shout and from the motorboat's cabin a man appears. He stares then turns his boat towards them. "It's silly to play out here on a raft . . ." he begins. "But we're not playing!" Rupert protests. "We're escaping from pirates!" "Pirates!" the man repeats. "Now that's enough of your nonsense." "Oh, please, we are telling the truth!" Rupert pleads. The pals sound

so earnest that at last the man takes them in tow, saying that he is taking them to the police station to tell their story.

The policeman who hears their tale does not seem to believe it. "You come from Nutwood, eh?" he frowns. "I know P.C. Growler there. I shall ring and ask him about you. Pirates, indeed! What will some of you youngsters think of next!" And with that he dials the number of Nutwood police station. The pals wait anxiously.

18

RUPERT HELPS THE POLICE

"Your village bobby says that I
Should take your word. You never lie."

So in the police car off they go
To let the river bobbies know.

The pals are asked to show the way.
"A police boat ride! Of course!" they say.

Tom's seen them, waved, the waters race.
They're dragged towards the tunnel place.

"H'm, is that a fact?" The policeman listens to P.C. Growler in Nutwood. He puts down the 'phone. "Well," he says, "it seems that neither of you tells lies, so I've got to believe this extraordinary tale about pirates on the river. Oh, dear! What are the River Police going to say about this? Well, come on! Let's go and find out." With that he leads the pals out to his police car and sets off for the Nutchester River Police station.

The River Police act at once when they hear what has happened to Rupert and Bingo. Will Rupert and Bingo come with them and show just where they were trapped in their boat? Of course! Who's going to turn down the chance of a trip in a River Police boat? So off they go. As they get near the tunnel leading to the mill Rupert and Bingo spot Young Tom at his lookout post. Already he is signalling. "Look out!" Rupert calls. Too late. The water is swirling!

RUPERT FINDS HIS PALS

"*Quick, duck your heads. The roof is low!*"
Too late. Police helmets flying go.

Up comes the net. Ben groans, "Oh, dear!
We've really caught the wrong lot here."

Tom rushes down to see his prize,
Gets close and can't believe his eyes.

Then at a window Rupert spies
Two faces. "They're our pals!" he cries.

Before the policemen know what's happening their boat is being dragged into the tunnel. "Watch your heads!" Rupert cries. Again too late. Helmets go flying! The police boat is swept through the tunnel by the current. This time Rupert and Bingo know what to expect and they are ready for the shock when the net brings the craft to a jolting halt. Being large and heavy the two policeman avoid being sent sprawling. There is a long silence.

Ben breaks the silence. "Oh, dear!" he squeaks. "We've really caught the wrong lot here!" Just then Tom hurries down to see what he's trapped. For an awe-stricken moment he regards the scene. "I really must get glasses," he says at last.

It is while the pirates are being rounded up that Rupert happens to look up at the loft windows. "Bingo!" he cries. "Look who's there!" Grinning down at them from the loft they left such a short time ago are – Bill and Algy.

RUPERT MAKES A PLEA

Algy explains that Bill and he
Were captured as their pals got free.

Then off the police – and pirates – go
With Rupert and his chums in tow.

Now Rupert asks the policeman, "Please
Don't punish them." And he agrees.

As once again our chums set out,
"Good luck and thanks!" the pirates shout.

"Bill! Algy!" Rupert and Bingo run to greet the two captives who have just been let out of the loft. "They caught us just as you and Bingo were escaping," laughs Algy. "They seemed quite upset that you'd gone after they'd given you supper and the like." "I know," Rupert says. "They're awful pirates because they're kind." Just then one of the policemen calls, "Back to Nutchester." And off they go, the police boat with the pirates in it, towing the other two.

At the River Police station Rupert goes up to one of the policemen. "They're not really bad," he begins. "I know," says the policeman. "We'll find a place for them in the Rocky Bay Home for Retired Pirates." So Rupert and the others can set out again quite happily. As they leave, the old pirates wave after them. "Good luck!" they call. "Have a good holiday and do come and see us sometime!" The End.

RUPERT and

"Please tell me, if you'd be so kind,
Where my mate Sailor Sam I'll find."

"Ahoy there, young bear!" Rupert who is enjoying a walk on Nutwood Common turns to see a cheerful looking man dressed like a sailor. "I'm looking for the home of an old shipmate of mine named Sam," he says. Rupert smiles. "Sailor Sam is a friend of mine, too," he says. "I'll show you the way." The sailor thanks him and soon Rupert is pointing out Sam's trim cabin on top of a rise.

the WORG SEEDS

"Sam," Rupert says, "is my friend too.
His shack I'll gladly take you to."

Sam scarcely can believe his eyes.
His mouth drops open with surprise.

When Sam answers Rupert's knock at the door and sees the chubby figure standing beside him his mouth drops open with surprise and for a moment he can't speak. Then he bursts out, "Bill! I haven't seen you in ages. Oh, this is grand!" He turns to Rupert. "This here's my good old shipmate Bill Bottle. Him and me sailed together for many a year. What luck he bumped into you, another good friend."

"This here's Bill Bottle. Him and me
For years together sailed the sea."

23

RUPERT GETS A PRESENT

"Since you were kind to help me so,
Please take this gift before you go."

"Witchdoctors," Bill says, "far away
Use just such rattles every day."

"Hey, Bingo!" Rupert cries. "See what
A most unusual gift I've got."

"It must have had a lot of use,
For, see, this plug is coming loose."

Rupert can see that the two old shipmates have a lot to talk about so he says that he must be off home. But Bill Bottle asks him to wait a moment. He rummages in his kitbag and produces a brightly painted object shaped rather like a coconut. "For you for being such a help," he says and hands it to Rupert. "Oh, thank you!" Rupert gasps. "But – what is it?" Bill laughs: "It's a rattle such as witchdoctors in far off places use." Delighted, Rupert starts for home

to show off his strange present. But on the way he sees Bingo posting a letter and just has to show him the rattle and tell him what it is. "A witchdoctor's rattle!" Bingo cries. "Do let's have a go." So Rupert hands it over. Bingo studies the strange painting on it then shakes it. It gives out a dry rattle as if there were little beads or stones in it. "I say," says Bingo after a moment, "it must have had a lot of use. This plug in the end is loose."

RUPERT SWALLOWS THE SEEDS

He peers and shakes it all about,
But still can't make the rattlers out.

He lifts it for a better view.
Before he knows, he's swallowed two!

"Quick, fetch the doctor!" Rupert pleads.
"I've swallowed some odd sort of seeds."

"Now take this dose. Sleep well tonight.
I'm sure you're going to be all right."

Rupert is about to push the plug back securely when Bingo says, "Take it out for a moment and try to see what makes the rattling sound." So Rupert removes the plug and peers into the hole, shaking the contents gently. It is so dark he can see nothing. He raises it above his head to let light in. But he turns it over too far just as he opens his mouth to speak – and two seedlike things drop into it. Before he can stop himself he has swallowed them!

In no time at all Rupert is rushing into his garden crying, "Oh, fetch the doctor. I've just swallowed some odd seeds!" When Mrs. Bear hears what has happened she decides that calling Dr. Lion would be safer. So a little later Rupert is tucked up in bed and Dr. Lion is giving him a dose of medicine. "I don't think there's any need to worry," Dr. Lion says. "But I'll give you this medicine to be on the safe side. Then have a good rest and I'll call tomorrow."

RUPERT WAKES UP SHRUNK

At first next morning Mrs. Bear
Can't see her Rupert anywhere.

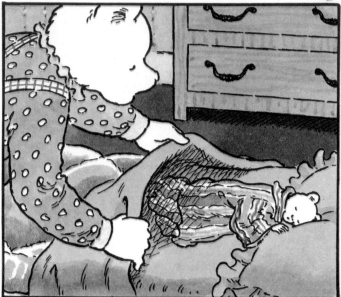

Then she looks close and there he lies,
But shrunk to less than half his size!

"This really is an awful shame!
Those seeds I swallowed are to blame."

"Of potions, spells and such as those,
The Wise Old Goat's the one who knows."

Rupert sleeps well that night. But something is happening to him as he sleeps. He dreams the blankets are too heavy and his pyjamas too big. He is still asleep when Mrs. Bear comes to waken him next day. At first she thinks his bed is empty. But when she pulls back the blankets she gasps and gives a groan of dismay. "Oh, Rupert, whatever has happened to you?" she cries. For during the night Rupert has shrunk to a fraction of his normal size!

Rupert can't believe what has happened to him. Wrapped in a big handkerchief – for his clothes are miles too big – he wails, "Those wretched seeds have done this!" And that's what Dr. Lion decides too when he is called. But what is he to do? He has never come across anything like this. Then Rupert has an idea. His mysterious friend the Wise Old Goat who lives near Nutwood knows a lot about spells and potions. "I'll call him and ask his advice right away," says Dr. Lion.

RUPERT HEARS ABOUT THE SEEDS

Off Dr. Lion goes to call
The Wise Old Goat and tell him all.

"He knows those very seeds and says
You'll grow again in, say, two days."

"I'll make some things for you to wear
Until you grow," says Mrs. Bear.

He tries to draw and play and such,
But everything weighs far too much.

Taking the rattle and its seeds, Dr. Lion goes to call the Wise Old Goat. "I do hope I won't stay this size," Rupert sighs. "I'm sure it won't last," Mrs. Bear comforts him. And that is Dr. Lion's good news when he returns. "The Wise Old Goat," he says, "knows the seeds. They are called Worg seeds – the name is the opposite of 'grow' – and the Goat says you will be back to normal size in a couple of days. Meanwhile it is safer to stay indoors."

Rupert is much happier now he knows he won't stay tiny. He even enjoys the novelty of his new size, wearing a toy soldier's uniform while Mrs. Bear makes him little clothes and even boots. But the novelty wears off. His toys are all too big for him. So are books. As for pencils and painting brushes, they're much too heavy he finds. And making things even more boring is having to stay indoors, although he does realise it's for his own safety.

RUPERT'S PAL SPOTS DANGER

For Rupert's meals his parents get
A tiny doll's house dining set.

"I do so wish I might go out,"
He thinks. Then hears a friendly shout.

"Oh, Bingo, I'm so glad you've come!"
He cries and runs to greet his chum.

But Bingo shouts, "Oh, do take care!"
And points at something in the air.

Next morning Rupert is still as small as ever. But Mrs. Bear reminds him that Dr. Lion has said that, according to the Wise Old Goat, he will start to grow quite quickly and suddenly. While he eats breakfast at a doll's dining set Mrs. Bear has borrowed, she reminds him that he may start growing again any time. "You wouldn't want to burst out of your clothes outside," she says. Rupert laughs. But the sun is shining and soon he is standing wistfully at the front door wishing he could go out. Then a familiar figure comes through the gate. "Bingo!" Rupert cries. "I'm so glad you've come. It's boring having to stay indoors." Delightedly he runs to greet his chum. "My goodness, you are small!" Bingo says. "We heard what happened to you after swallowing those seeds but . . . ." He breaks off and points over Rupert's head. "Rupert, look out!" he cries. Rupert hears a swishing sound. He turns and gasps with dismay.

RUPERT TAKES TO THE AIR

"No, no!" poor Rupert cries in dread.
A jackdaw hovers overhead.

Rupert's chum dashes from the gate
To scare the bird – alas, too late!

How Mrs. Bear wails in dismay
To see her Rupert swept away.

At last the jackdaw comes to rest,
With Rupert held above its nest.

Horrified, Rupert sees a huge bird swooping on him. Well, it's huge to poor Rupert even though it is just an ordinary jackdaw. To him it looks big and fierce. He tries to rush back indoors but the jackdaw is on him. Bingo rushes at it shouting, and Mrs. Bear hurries to the door to see what all the fuss is. Both are too late. "Oh, please, no!" cries Rupert as the jackdaw scoops him up. "Oh, Rupert!" Mrs. Bear wails. Bingo waves his arms and shouts, "Come back here with my pal!" But the jackdaw has Rupert's jersey firmly in its beak and carries him out of the garden, high among the trees. Rupert is too shocked to say anything. He just keeps hoping that the bird does not let go of him. At last the bird swoops at an old wall. Rupert thinks they are going to fly straight into it. Then he spies a nest tucked into a hole in the wall and a moment later finds himself being dangled over it.

RUPERT IS DUMPED IN A NEST

It peers at him as if to see
What this bright wriggling thing might be.

"You can't leave me here!" Rupert cries,
When from the nest the jackdaw flies.

"Oh, dear, if I were not so small
I could just step down from this wall."

"Among those things I think I see
One that will be of use to me."

Gently, the jackdaw sets Rupert in the nest. Trembling, he waits to see what the bird means to do with him. But it only studies him, puzzled by this brightly coloured wriggling thing it has added to its collection. And what a collection! A thimble, old nails, a broken comb and lots more. Suddenly the bird flaps its wings and flies off. "Hey, you can't leave me here like this!" Rupert shouts. But it does, and disappears over the trees.

"Well, there's only one thing for it," Rupert tells himself. "I must escape on my own." He peers over the edge of the nest. Little more than a step to the ground if he were his normal size. Now it looks quite frightening. "Somehow, I must get away before the bird comes back," he thinks. "But how? If only I had some rope then I could climb down." Then as he gazes around the jackdaw's collection in the nest he spots something he can use.

RUPERT TRIES TO ESCAPE

"This ball of yarn is strong, I hope.
I mean to use it as a rope."

One end's tied to a branch that's sound.
The rest is heaved down to the ground.

There is no time to hang about.
He grasps the yarn and scrambles out.

A sound of wings. He turns to stare.
The bird's returning to its lair.

What Rupert has spotted is a ball of yarn. At some time its colour must have caught the bird's eye, and that's reason enough for a jackdaw to steal anything. Rupert knots one end of the yarn to a stout twig growing above the nest. He tugs it to make sure it's strong enough then pushes the ball of yarn to the side of the nest. Although it seems big to him, it is quite light and he easily heaves it over the side. It unwinds as it falls.

Once more Rupert tugs the yarn to be sure it is strong enough. Then holding it tightly he scrambles over the side of the nest and begins his descent. The wall isn't high but to Rupert it is like a cliff. Once his feet slip and he hangs in space. But he manages to wrap his legs round the yarn and climbs on down, hand over hand. There is still some way to go when he hears a flapping sound. He looks up with a start. The jackdaw is returning!

RUPERT FINDS MORE TROUBLE

The bird is coming fast and so
He has no choice but to let go.

He hasn't far to drop at all.
A big soft tussock breaks his fall.

"I need some place the bird can't see.
Ah, yes. The hole beneath that tree."

He stumbles. There's a rumbling sound.
Next thing he's falling through the ground.

Rupert clings to the yarn not daring to move. The bird seems not to have seen him for it circles slowly. What is he to do? Stay still, hoping the bird doesn't spot him and flies away? Or carry on, hoping he reaches the ground before it reaches him? Then his mind is made up for him. Suddenly the jackdaw does see him. It swoops. It is coming fast. It is only inches away, its beak angrily open. There's only one thing for it. Rupert lets go – and hopes!

Luckily he was pretty near the ground when he let go and he lands softly on a big tussock of grass. At once he scrambles deep into the long grass to hide. For what seems ages the jackdaw circles above. But at last it gives up and flies off. Rupert looks round for a place to rest while he decides what to do. He picks a hole between the roots of a tree. As he runs into it he trips and falls against a sort of twig. The ground drops from under his feet.

RUPERT JUST SAVES HIMSELF

He's tumbled through a sort of hatch.
He sees a ladder. Makes a snatch.

He grabs the ladder safely but
The hatch that he fell through slams shut.

He climbs back up but just to prove
He cannot get the hatch to move.

"No way out there. So down I'll go
And see what I can find below."

Rupert gives a cry as the ground drops from under him. He tries to grab the twig he fell against. He misses and finds himself falling down a shaft. He catches a glimpse of a rope ladder and grabs at it. He gets it, but with a jolt that knocks the breath out of him. He scrabbles with his feet for a foothold. Then as he clings trembling to the ladder there is a "clump" and the trapdoor he has fallen through – for that's what is is – slams shut.

"What a day!" Rupert thinks as he clings to the ladder. "First that wretched jackdaw and now this! Well, I can't stay here." So up the ladder he starts to see if he can open the trapdoor. But try as he may he can't budge it. "There must be some way of opening it from the inside but I can't find it," he pants. Then he notices a glow from the bottom of the shaft. "Right," he decides, "if I can't go up I'll go down. Maybe there's a way out down there."

RUPERT TRIES A DOOR

He finds a passage brightly lit
And thinks, "I'd better follow it."

He feels he's seen this place before.
Then just ahead he spots a door.

He tiptoes up and cocks an ear.
"What is that snorting sound I hear?"

"It's snoring," breathes the little bear.
"There's someone fast asleep in there."

As Rupert starts to pick his way carefully down the ladder a thought strikes him. It's about the size of the ladder. "It fits me," he thinks. "Whoever put it there must be little, like me now." The glow from the bottom of the shaft gets brighter as he descends. The ladder ends at some steps down to a passage lit by lanterns. It seems familiar as he starts along it. He listens hard for any sound. Then a little way ahead he sees a door.

"Who – or what – is behind it?" he wonders. He studies it from a distance. At last he tells himself, "Well, I can't just stand here doing nothing. I'll have to try it." Cautiously he tiptoes to it. Then he puts his ear to it and, holding his breath, listens. What he hears is a snorty sort of sound. What can it be? Then there is one very loud snort and Rupert knows what it is. Someone is snoring in there! Carefully he turns the handle and pushes.

RUPERT CAN'T WAKEN THE IMPS

He steals inside. "Now, there's a thing!
I know them well – the Imps of Spring!"

He gives each Imp a gentle shake,
But no one seems to want to wake.

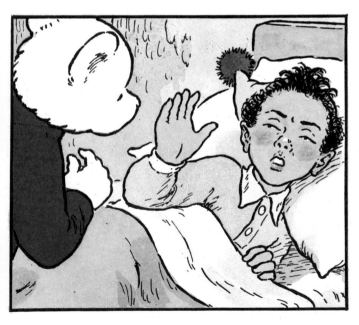

One Imp does stir and with a sigh
Says, "'Tisn't Spring yet, so goodbye!"

"No rousing them so let's explore.
I say, what's this? Another door."

Rupert peers into the room. He gasps. It is a large room with beds down each side. In them are little figures he knows well having met them several times. The Imps of Spring! The creatures who waken the countryside after its winter sleep. In a big bed at the end lies their King – still wearing his crown! "No wonder I thought that passage was familiar!" Rupert thinks. "I'll just waken one of the Imps and ask how I get out of here." But rousing a slumbering Imp of Spring is not that easy. From bed to bed he goes gently shaking its occupant's shoulder. But they are too fast asleep even to stir. All except one, that is. And he only opens one eye long enough to mumble, "'Tisn't Spring yet. So goodbye." Then he is asleep again. Rupert doesn't fancy trying the Imps' King. At the best of times he is short-tempered. He returns to the passage. Further along he finds a door marked STORES.

RUPERT SURPRISES THE TROLLS

From inside Rupert hears the sound
Of something smashing on the ground.

Inside he finds strange creatures who
Are stealing the Imps' honeydew.

"Hey, stop that!" cries the little bear.
The strangers jump. They turn and stare.

Then, "Get him, Trolls!" their leader cries
As down the passage Rupert flies.

Rupert decides to try the door. Maybe there is someone inside who can help him. Perhaps he can find something to eat for he is beginning to feel really hungry. He reaches the door and is about to open it when he hears a crash from behind it. Quietly he opens the door. He gasps at what he sees. Strange little creatures with long whiskers are loading a trolley with the Imps' honeydew. Rupert sees what caused the sound he heard. A broken jar lies on the floor.

Rupert is too amazed to speak. And the little creatures are too busy to notice him. "They're stealing it!" Rupert tells himself. "The Imps need that honeydew to build their strength in the Spring after their long sleep." Then not thinking what might happen, he shouts, "You can't do that!" The little creatures freeze. They turn and stare. For a second no one moves. Then Rupert turns and races down the passage. "Get him, Trolls!" he hears the cry.

RUPERT ROUSES THE IMPS

"Help! Help!" the Imps hear Rupert shout.
They rouse themselves and tumble out.

In hardly any time at all
The Imps have captured every Troll.

The King surveys the sorry crew,
And Rupert asks him what he'll do.

"You found them, little bear, so I'd
Much rather that you should decide."

Rupert hasn't stopped to think where he is going, only that he must get away. Although they are dumpy the Trolls run fast and Rupert hears them getting closer. "Help! Help!" he shouts as he runs. His cries and the noise of the chase are so loud that they waken the Imps from their sleep. Suddenly the passage is full of angry Imps who burst out of their bedroom. There is a scuffle and the Trolls are all overpowered.

Now the King of the Imps appears. The Trolls are lined up for him. "They all look alike!" Rupert gasps. "You can't tell one from the other," the King agrees. 'Not that it makes any difference. They're all troublesome, wandering about underground living off what they can find – no matter whose it is." The Trolls look so sad that Rupert feels rather sorry for them. "What will you do with them?" he asks the King. "You found them so you decide," the King says.

37

RUPERT LETS THE TROLLS GO

"Please let us go and this I swear,
We'll never steal again, young bear."

"I do believe him, sire, and so
I think that we should let them go."

As soon as all the Trolls have gone
The Imps begin to stretch and yawn.

"Hey!" Rupert cries. "Before you go,
How I get out I've got to know."

The King's decree takes Rupert completely by surprise. "Oh, dear," he thinks, "What shall I do?" All the time the Trolls are gazing at him pleadingly. Then one of them speaks: "We meant no harm, young sir. There are no sweet things in our mountain home, and we all so love honeydew. Please let us go. We promise never to steal again." He looks so contrite that Rupert tells the King, "I really do believe he means it, sire. I think we should let them go."

The King does not look pleased at Rupert's decision. But he has given his word that Rupert should decide what happens to the Trolls. "Let them go!" he orders his Imps. Looking none too pleased themselves, they release the Trolls. After a quick "Thank you" to Rupert the Trolls set off up the passage and the Imps, yawning, troop back into their bedroom. As the last one disappears, Rupert calls after them, "Hey, what about me? How do I get out of here?"

RUPERT IS LEFT ALL ALONE

But not an Imp can Rupert wake
To tell him which way he should take.

So Rupert ventures off alone
To find a way out on his own.

Ahead of him he spots the Trolls.
"Hey, wait for me, you lot!" he calls.

"We hope you haven't come to say
You've changed your mind and we must stay."

The Trolls have gone. The Imps have returned to bed. And Rupert is alone underground. He must do something. So he goes back into the Imps' bedroom where he has as much luck wakening them as he did before. This time he even tries the King. But the tiny ruler only half-opens an eye and mumbles, "Shouldn't be awake at all this time of year. . . ." then falls fast asleep again. Rupert returns to the passage. He knows he can't get out the way he got in so he sets off the other way, hoping he might come across some exit to the outside world. He hears footsteps ahead and spies several small figures. "The Trolls, of course!" he thinks. "They know their way about under the earth." He hurries after them. "Hey, Trolls!" he cries. "Please wait for me!' To his relief the little creatures do stop and wait for him to catch up. But when he reaches them his heart sinks. They look so stern.

RUPERT IS LED TO THE OUTSIDE

"Oh, no," says Rupert. "Have no fear.
I just want to get out of here."

"You've been so kind we'll show you where
There is an exit, little bear."

The way out is no size at all,
And Rupert's glad he's still so small.

"Nutwood village! So there you are!"
The Troll says. "And it isn't far."

The Trolls may look alike but one appears to be the leader. He speaks and Rupert learns the reason for the stern looks. "You haven't changed your mind about letting us go?" he asks. "Of course not!" Rupert cries. "I just want to ask you to help me get back to the outside world and my home in Nutwood." "That we shall!" says the Troll. "You're the only one who's ever been kind to us. Come on, there is a way out just a little way on from here."

With that the Trolls set out at a brisk pace, Rupert trotting along with them. After a while they come to a steep and narrow stairway. The Troll leader starts up it and Rupert, panting by now, follows. "It's just as well I'm as small as I am," he thinks when, at the top, he sees the little hole that leads to the outside world. Then he is outside with the Troll leader who points to the lights of Nutwood and says, "There you are!"

RUPERT GETS A LIFT HOME

"It isn't all that far, I know.
But I'm so small I'm scared to go."

"Then," says the Troll, "what we must do
Is make a frame and carry you."

And so he's borne home unafraid
Upon the frame the Trolls have made.

The Trolls make sure that he's all right
Then disappear into the night.

"Well, goodbye then," says the Troll leader. "Oh, please," pleads Rupert. "Don't go yet!" "Why, isn't that Nutwood?" the Troll asks. "Y-yes," Rupert falters. "But I'm so small I'm scared of going all that way alone." Then he explains about the Worg seeds and his adventure with the jackdaw. The Troll thinks a moment then snaps a series of orders at the others. They bustle about collecting twigs and plaiting them into a sort of mat. "We'll carry you home," announces the Troll leader. "Climb on." So Rupert takes his place on the mat. Four Trolls lift it to their shoulders and off they go. "What a grand way to travel!" Rupert laughs. "Quiet!" he is told. "We don't want anyone to see us." So with Rupert whispering directions the Trolls bear him to Nutwood and his own door. "Goodbye and thanks," he whispers. The little creatures all wave and vanish into the darkness. Rupert knocks at the door.

RUPERT IS HIS OLD SIZE AGAIN

"Oh, Mummy, it's been such a day
Since that bird carried me away!"

"My dear, your clothes are far too tight.
I'm sure that you have grown tonight."

He's overjoyed next morning when
He finds he's his old size again.

"Hey, you there, jackdaw in the tree!
I don't think you remember me!"

Mr. and Mrs. Bear are overjoyed to have their tiny son back. "How did you get away from that bird?" they ask. "First, could I please have some supper?" Rupert laughs. "I'm starving!" While he tucks into a meal he tells them all about his adventures.

Later as he is going to bed, his clothes begin to feel very tight. "I've eaten too much," he says. "No!" Mummy laughs. "You have begun to grow again! Isn't that splendid!"

Next morning Rupert jumps out of bed, puts on a dressing gown – his normal size one – and stands before the mirror. "I'm my right size!" he shouts with delight. He is so very excited he can scarcely eat his breakfast and the moment it is over he dashes out to play. As he races down the garden path on his scooter he sees a bird on a branch. "It's the same jackdaw, I'm sure!" he gasps. Laughing, he shakes a fist at the puzzled bird. The End.

Rupert's Paper Crown

Follow these simple instructions to make Rupert's Paper Crown. Trim a double page from a small-size newspaper to a square. Fold the opposite corners together to give the diagonal creases which will be your centre lines. These are important so be sure you get them exact.

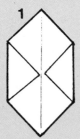 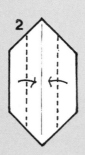 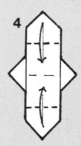 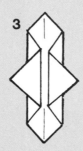 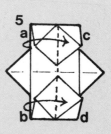

Fold opposite corners to centre as in 1. Turn the paper over and fold sides to middle as in 2, letting points pop out from behind to give 3. Turn the paper over and fold top and bottom points to the middle as in 4. Now fold side AB to CD as in 5 to give you 6.

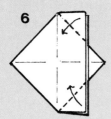 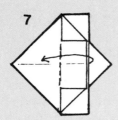 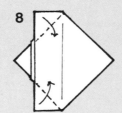 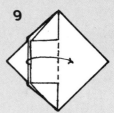

Fold the corners, top layer only, as shown in 6. Then bring over both layers as shown by the arrow in 7. Fold the corners as shown in 8. Now fold back the top layer only as in 9 to give you 10. Be sure all your folds and creases are firm and neat.

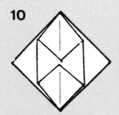 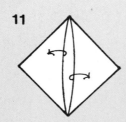 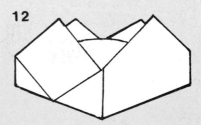

Turn the paper over and open out as shown in 11 by gently pulling apart the edges at the centre to make it 3D. Now you have 12, Rupert's Paper Crown. Why not try out the instructions first with a large sheet of typing paper trimmed to a square?

RUPERT and

Rupert is running home for tea
When someone calls behind a tree.

Rupert who has been playing on the common with his chums is hurrying home before it gets dark and wondering whether there will be muffins for tea. Then "Psst! Hey, Rupert!" a little voice calls. Rupert stops and looks around. "Here in the bushes," the voice adds. In the fading light Rupert makes out a figure he knows well, Santa Claus's helper, the little cowboy – not looking his happy self.

the LOTUS ISLE

A little cowboy's there. What's more
An airplane he has seen before.

It's Santa's helper, but it's clear
He wants no one to know he's here.

"What are you doing here?" Rupert calls. The cowboy doesn't answer but beckons Rupert to him. "What's all this about?" Rupert asks. "Ssh!" hushes the cowboy. "I don't want everyone to know I'm here." Rupert stares at him, wondering why he is so serious. Usually he's a very cheerful little soul. The cowboy looks all around to make sure no one can hear then asks, "Have you seen Santa Claus around here, huh?"

The cowboy whispers, looking grim,
"Santa, Rupert – have you seen him?"

When Rupert asks the cowboy why
He wants to know, there's no reply.

"Oh, gee! You'd better know. It's weird.
Santa has simply disappeared!"

"Each year 'round now he likes to go
And check his Christmas route, you know."

"This year he's not come back again.
So I've been searching in my 'plane."

Rupert stares at the little cowboy. It is such an odd question. The cowboy, looking badly worried, repeats it. "Have you seen Santa?" "But why would Santa be here now?" Rupert asks. "He doesn't come 'til Christmas." The little cowboy's answer is a deep sigh. "Gee, I don't know whether I should tell even you," he groans. "Maybe if you did I could help," Rupert suggests. "Right," says the cowboy, "Here goes! The fact is, Santa has disappeared!"

"Disappeared? Santa?" Rupert repeats as if he can't believe his ears. The cowboy nods glumly and sinks wearily onto a big stone. "Each year around now Santa makes a practice run round the route he'll take at Christmas, looking for any possible snags. Well, this year he went off as usual. But he hasn't returned. He should've been back days ago. I've been searching for him in my 'plane." He points to his machine which he has hidden in some bushes.

RUPERT LEARNS WHERE SANTA IS

"That's our carrier pigeon, see!
Maybe it's got some news for me."

The cowboy runs to meet the bird.
And as he thought, it's brought some word.

"A reindeer has returned to say
He's on some isle and means to stay."

"I've got to fetch him, little bear.
This pigeon here will show me where."

"What do you think has happened to him?" asks Rupert. "Don't know," the cowboy sighs. "But, sure thing, if he don't get back soon a lot of people ain't gonna get Christmas presents. He's the only one who knows who gets what . . ." He breaks off at the sound of flapping wings and looks up. "Hey, that's one of our messenger pigeons!" he says. "It must have something for me." He jumps up waving his arms and runs to meet the pigeon as it swoops to the ground.

He takes a strip of paper from a tube on the pigeon's leg and reads it. He whistles at what it says. "One of Santa's reindeer has come back to his castle with a strange story. Santa's on some island not caring that Christmas is near. He and the reindeer just doze in the sun and eat some kinda local fruit. The only reason this reindeer came back is 'cos it hates fruit. I'm ordered to fly to that island and bring them back. The pigeon will show me where."

47

RUPERT AGREES TO HELP

"This could be tough. Sure would be grand
If you'd come too and lend a hand."

Rupert is keen but has to know
If Mrs. Bear will let him go.

Mummy agrees but thinks it best
The two should have a good night's rest.

At dawn they're up and off again
To where the cowboy left his 'plane.

"Gee, this sure could be a tough job," the cowboy muses. "Getting Santa and the reindeer back if they don't wanna come." He pauses then adds, "Sure would be grand if you'd come and help me." Rupert is taken aback. "Well, yes, I suppose . . ." he stammers. "Great! I knew you would!" the cowboy cries. "Hey, wait," Rupert says. "I shall have to ask Mummy." "Then let's do that!" urges the cowboy. So leaving the bird to look after the 'plane, the two hurry off.

At home Rupert lets the cowboy explain. "Please, do say yes!" Rupert pleads. "It would be dreadful if Santa wasn't back in time for Christmas." Mrs. Bear looks at Mr. Bear who nods. "Very well," she says. "You may go with the cowboy – when you've had a good night's sleep." So a bed is made up for the cowboy in Rupert's room and next day very early they get up, breakfast and hurry to where the airplane is waiting – and, of course, the pigeon.

RUPERT GOES BY AIR

The pigeon shows our two the way
As they set off at break of day.

Their first look at their goal they take.
An island in a mountain lake.

They find a place where they can land
Along a stretch of tree-fringed sand.

"There's someone lying over there.
I think we've found him, little bear!"

The sun is rising over Nutwood as Rupert and the cowboy set off. The pigeon leads the way. As the sun gets higher the land is left behind and they find themselves flying over the ocean. On they go with the sky getting clearer and the weather warmer. Then the bird climbs and the 'plane follows. Rupert soon sees why. They are crossing mountains whose peaks poke through the clouds. Amid the mountains lies a lake – with an island in it!

When they are clear of the peaks the bird swoops towards the island with the 'plane close behind. It leads the way to a beach where the 'plane can land safely. The cowboy switches off the engine and he and Rupert climb down and look around them. Everything is warm and bright. It's hard to believe they were in wintry Nutwood so recently. Then – "Look!" the cowboy whispers and points to where, in the distance, someone is lying under a sunshade.

RUPERT FINDS SANTA

Indeed it's Santa, even though
He's not dressed in the way they know.

"I do so like this place. And you,"
He says, "I hope will like it too."

The cowboy cries, "We can't stay here!
Christmas is getting very near."

"Don't fuss," says Santa with a smile.
"Try one. They're special to this isle."

Quietly Rupert and the cowboy approach the figure under the sunshade. Yes, it is Santa all right! At first glance it's hard to recognise him for neither of the pair has ever seen him like this before. No familiar fur-trimmed red hood and tunic. No big boots. But rolled up shirt sleeves and bare feet. Yet it's him. He seems to be dozing, but he stirs and reaches out a lazy arm for a piece of fruit from a dish by his side. He spots Rupert and the cowboy but, although his eyes widen for a moment as if he wonders why they are there, he doesn't rise. He bites into the juicy fruit and drawls, "It's so nice here. I do hope you'll enjoy it too." "We can't stay here!" cries the cowboy. "It's nearly Christmas and you should have been back ages ago!" "Christmas," repeats Santa. "Ah, yes. No reason to fuss." He smiles lazily. "Here, try some of this fruit. We discovered them when we stopped here to rest. They are delicious!"

RUPERT HEARS ABOUT THE FRUIT

The cowboy takes the fruit and tries.
Says, "Mm! It's nice." And shuts his eyes.

Next thing he's stretched out, Santa too.
Rupert's left wondering what to do.

"The fruit's to blame," thinks Rupert Bear.
"They eat it then don't seem to care."

The pigeon says, "So long as they
Keep eating it they'll stay that way."

"Come on, Santa!" the cowboy pleads. "Don't you understand what I'm saying? Christmas is so near and you've got so much to do!" But Santa just smiles sleepily and murmurs, "Calm down. Enjoy the sunshine. Eat your lovely fruit." Almost absent-mindedly the cowboy accepts the fruit which looks like a ripe golden peach, takes a bite and chews. He hasn't swallowed more than a couple of mouthfuls when he yawns and stretches out on the sand beside Santa.

"Not you too!" Rupert groans. But the cowboy is asleep. "It was so sudden," Rupert mutters. "He was eating . . ." He stops. "That's it!" he cries. "The fruit's doing this to them!" "You're right," a voice chips in. It's the pigeon. "Birds won't eat that fruit," it adds. "They'd never find their way home if they did. And I can tell you, those two will stay like this as long as they eat it." "Why didn't you tell us?" cries Rupert. "No one asked," replies the silly bird.

RUPERT IS BADLY WORRIED

The two stir, eat some fruit and then
They both go back to sleep again.

"I must have help. Do go and see
If there's someone who can aid me."

"If I can't get them out of here
There'll be no Christmas gifts this year."

"There's only Santa's reindeer here,
And they're all fast asleep, I fear."

"Can't we stop them eating the fruit?" Rupert asks the pigeon. "Can't see how," it says. "It tastes so nice they'll want to go on eating it. And there's so much of it growing here." The sleepers stir and reach for the fruit. "No!" cries Rupert. Too late. They bite, swallow and settle back to doze. Nothing Rupert can do rouses them. "I must get help," he says. He turns to the bird. "You can start by seeing if there's anyone on the island who might help."

The pigeon takes off over the trees and Rupert settles on the sand to think. His thoughts are really worrying. If he can't wake Santa and the cowboy and get them to leave, no one is going to get Christmas presents. The bird returns. It has spotted Santa's reindeer and sleigh. But the reindeer too have been gorging the fruit and are sleeping soundly. "I saw no sign of anyone," says the pigeon. "Then I must think of something," vows Rupert. "But what?"

RUPERT IS GIVEN ADVICE

*"The Old Professor's the one who
Would know the sort of thing to do."*

*The bird says, "Take the 'plane and go
To see him. I the way will show."*

*"I've often seen the cowboy fly.
The least that I can do is try."*

*He starts. The beach goes flying past.
Next moment he is climbing fast.*

As he puzzles over how to get help Rupert begins to feel hungry. "And there's only that wretched fruit to eat," he thinks. "I can't eat that." This makes getting away all the more urgent. He sighs and says aloud: "If only my friend the Professor was here. He'd know what to do." The pigeon pipes up, "Since he's not here go and find him." "How?" Rupert demands. "Take the cowboy's 'plane," the bird replies. "I'll show you the way back to Nutwood."

Rupert stops on the point of telling the bird not to be silly and mutters, "I wonder . . . after all I've watched the cowboy fly. It looks pretty simple," "Have a try!" the bird urges. Rupert nods and a few moments later is climbing aboard the 'plane. He holds his breath and presses the button marked START. The engine roars. The propellor spins. The machine races along the beach. Rupert tugs the wheel that makes the 'plane go up and down. It starts to rise!

RUPERT LEARNS TO FLY

The pigeon guide just has to wait
While Rupert learns to fly quite straight.

But he soon gets it right and they
Are Nutwood bound and on their way.

"We're here now. So please fly down and
Tell me if it is clear to land."

"All clear," the pigeon says, and so
The flight is over. Down they go.

The little airplane is soon high over the sea. By pushing the wheel forward Rupert stops it climbing. But he can't stop flying in circles. Then he notices that his foot is pressing one of two pedals. When he takes his foot off it the 'plane stops turning. He pushes the other pedal and the 'plane turns the other way. Of course! The pedals steer the machine! He waves to show he is ready to start and soon the pigeon is leading him back over the high mountains.

Rupert thinks about the man he is flying home to ask for help. The Professor is a jolly old chap who lives in a tower near Nutwood with a little servant. He is good at inventing things and working out problems. Rupert sees the ocean give way to land then familiar countryside. And there's the Professor's tower. Rupert signs to the pigeon that he wants it to check if it is clear for him to land. It swoops down and comes back shortly to lead him to a smooth landing.

RUPERT TELLS THE PROFESSOR

The Old Professor hurries out
To see what all the row's about.

"It's lotus fruit. I know it well.
Your friends are captives of its spell."

"To their supply we'll soon put paid
With this machine that I have made."

"It harvests fruit at such a rush
The fruit ends up as nasty mush."

Rupert is taking from the airplane the fruit he has brought from the island when the Professor and his servant appear. They heard the plane land and are agog to know how and why Rupert has brought it here. Rupert tells his story then tucks into milk and sandwiches. The Professor examines the fruit. "Lotus fruit," he says. "When people fall under its spell the fruit has to be taken away from them." Then he adds with twinkle, "And I think I know how!"

The Professor leads the way to a big workshop. "That's how!" he says and points to a very odd airplane. "My harvicopter! It's a helicopter I invented for harvesting fruit." He shows Rupert a pipe under the machine. "This sucks up fruit and shoots it out of a funnel at the back into fruit basket gliders towed behind," he explains. Then he sighs: "But it sucks so hard it turns the fruit into mush . . . but that won't matter with lotus fruit, eh?"

RUPERT NOTICES A BOX

"We'll need this box to serve my plan,"
The Old Professor tells his man.

And then in just a little while
They're heading for the lotus isle.

The pigeon leading, they soon reach
The mountains and can see the beach.

They land on it and there they find
The scene that Rupert left behind.

"I see!" Rupert cries. "We scoop up all the lotus fruit then Santa and the others won't be able to eat any more!" The Professor chuckles: "I knew the harvicopter would come in useful one day." Then he and the servant bustle about getting the machine ready. While Rupert is opening the workshop doors he sees a box being loaded. Then in hardly any time at all he is in the air again sitting behind the Professor and with the servant following in the harvicopter.

Now it is back over the ocean with the pigeon leading. All the while Rupert keeps hoping that the Professor's plan will work and they will get Santa and the others away from the island in time for Christmas. It will be a miserable Christmas for a lot of children if they can't. Over the high peaks they fly to the lake with the lotus fruit island in the middle of it. Both airplanes swoop down to land on the beach where two figures lie.

RUPERT ASKS ABOUT THE BOX

The lotus eaters can't be stirred.
They smile, but neither says a word.

The old man cries, "No time to lose!
The harvicopter we must use!"

A moment later up they go,
Leaving the servant down below.

"What's in the box he has, you ask?
You'll find it helps us with our task."

Rupert and the others hurry along the beach to where Santa and the cowboy are stretched out. "I see what you mean," the Professor says to Rupert as he studies them. "They don't seem to have a care in the world." He tries to rouse the pair but the only response is drowsy smiles and a mumbled offer of lotus fruit before they drop off again. "Well," exclaims the Professor, "plainly there isn't a moment to lose. So let's get to the harvicopter, Rupert!"

Rupert has to trot to keep up with his friend as they make for the machine. The Professor gets into the pilot's seat. Rupert climbs in behind him. "Ready!" cries the Professor. He starts the engine, works the controls and the harvicopter lifts straight into the air. Rupert sees that the box he saw being loaded has been left with the servant and asks what it is. "It's something to make our task a bit easier," the Professor says with a smile. "You'll see."

RUPERT REAPS THE FRUIT

The harvicopter starts to gulp
The fruit and jet it out as pulp.

"There's Santa's reindeer and his sleigh.
My goodness, they are well away!"

"Let's hope they need no fruit 'til we
Have quite stripped every lotus tree."

"I've thought of that one, little bear,"
The old man says. "Just look down there."

"Now to get rid of all this wretched fruit!" the Professor shouts. He pulls a lever and the tube under the machine is lowered to the lotus trees. Then he pushes a button. There is a whining sound and all the fruit from one tree is sucked into the tube. From the tail of the machine there's a "whoosh!" and Rupert turns to see lotus fruit being sprayed out like marmalade mist. As the trees are cleared Rupert sees Santa's sleigh and the sleeping reindeer.

The harvicopter rapidly strips the trees of fruit and soon only those nearest Santa and the cowboy are left uncleared. "What happens if they re-fill their fruit dish before we've cleared the trees?" Rupert shouts, thinking how much longer that might keep the pair impossible to move. "They won't have to re-fill it," the Professor calls back. "I thought of that before we left home. Just take a look at what's happening on the beach." He points down at his servant and the slumbering figures.

RUPERT SEES THE PLAN WORK

They look like lotus fruit he's got
Inside the box. It seems they're not.

"They're very much alike but each
Is just an ordinary peach."

When no more lotus fruit remain
The harvicopter lands again.

The sleepers stir. They try a bite.
They know at once something's not right.

On the beach Rupert sees the servant between Santa and the cowboy. Beside him is the box the Professor has said would make it easier to get the two lotus fruit-eaters away from the island. He is piling something on the dish which held Santa's lotus fruit. Rupert looks harder. "He's putting more lotus fruit on the dish!" he cries. The Professor laughs. "Not lotus fruit," he calls. "Just ordinary peaches. But those two won't know . . . well, not at first!"

The last lotus tree is cleared. The Professor takes a final look round just to be sure then brings the harvicopter down on the beach. As he and Rupert approach Santa and the cowboy they see the pair stir. Each reaches drowsily for the fruit dish. Each bites into a fruit. Then again. And again. They abandon the fruit they are munching and try others but with the same result. By the time Rupert and the Professor reach them they are sitting up looking badly puzzled.

Now wide awake, Santa's aghast
To learn quite how much time has past.

He feels worse when he sees how deep
His reindeer are still sunk in sleep.

"Take Rupert, fly back and explain
Santa will soon be home again."

"And, Santa, I've thought of a way
Of moving both you and your sleigh."

Santa and the cowboy start to wake. At first they remember nothing. When they learn how the lotus fruit made them forget – or not care – about the work they had to do before Christmas, Santa groans: "Don't say we've slept through Christmas!" "No," says the Professor. "But you'll have to get a move on!" "Then, quick!" Santa cries. "My sleigh! My reindeer!" But when they go to where Rupert saw them from the air they find the animals fast asleep.

Nothing will waken the reindeer. It's clear they have eaten an awful lot of lotus fruit. So how is Santa to get his sleigh back to his castle in time? "Quite simply" says the Professor. He addresses the little cowboy: "You and Rupert fly to Santa's castle in your airplane. Tell them Santa will be there soon and to get everything ready." "But what about me and my sleigh?" Santa repeats. "We shall see to that now," smiles the Professor. "Now off you little ones go!"

RUPERT BRINGS GOOD NEWS

"My old friend's such a clever man!
I knew he would produce some plan."

They see – still by the pigeon led –
Santa's cloud castle right ahead.

The Secretary, looking hot,
Runs out to see what news they've brought.

"It's OK. Santa's on his way.
Wait 'til you see what pulls his sleigh!"

As the cowboy's airplane takes off from the island Rupert looks back. Now he sees how the Professor means to get Santa's sleigh home for him. He and the servant are tying it to the tail of the harvicopter. Rupert chuckles, "He always thinks of something." Then he remembers that the Professor said the harvicopter was designed to tow things – fruit basket gliders.

On and on they fly until at last they see Santa's castle gleaming through the clouds.

The sound of the 'plane landing brings a very worried looking little man scurrying onto the terrace. He is Santa's Secretary and it is his job to make sure everything is ready on time. So it's no wonder he is worried. "Oh, please don't say you haven't found Santa!" he pleads. Rupert laughs, "But we have!" The Secretary can scarcely speak for joy. "He's on his way, and wait 'til you see what's pulling his sleigh instead of reindeer!" the cowboy tells him.

61

RUPERT GOES HOME

While Santa's helpers rush about
The cowboy gets spare reindeer out.

Then one and all burst into cheers
When Santa from a cloud appears.

"Goodbye and thank you!" Santa cries
As home the harvicopter flies.

The servant's bringing back in style
The reindeer from the lotus isle.

Now he knows Santa will be back very soon the Secretary darts back into the castle, snapping out orders to all the helpers. The cowboy goes off to the stables to get the spare reindeer ready. All round Rupert there is such a bustle as toys are sorted and put into sacks ready for loading onto Santa's sleigh. Then he hears the clatter of the harvicopter. Everyone looks up, and how they cheer when it emerges from the clouds pulling Santa in his sleigh!

Everyone gathers round to thank the Professor. "Thank Rupert," he replies and tells how Rupert found Santa then flew back on his own for help. So everyone thanks both of them, and, busy as he is, Santa takes time to stand and wave as the pair set off for home. On the way they meet the servant bringing Santa's reindeer back, having somehow at last got the creatures awake. As they pass, the Professor calls across, "Santa has agreed that the cowboy will fly you home!"

RUPERT TELLS HIS PALS

They're home. There's Nutwood down below.
And it feels cold enough for snow.

It starts as he gets to his gate.
"Oh, snow for Christmas. This is great!"

Next day they see the cowboy's 'plane
Bringing the servant home again.

"Rupert, you know what that's about.
So tell us all!" the others shout.

On the way home Rupert asks, "Do you think Santa will be ready in time for Christmas?" "I'm quite sure he will," replies the Professor. "But they'll all have to work even harder than they usually do just before Christmas. Have no fear, everyone will get presents."

At last Nutwood appears and in a little while the harvicopter has set Rupert down near his cottage. Just then it starts to snow. "Snow for Christmas! This is great!" Rupert laughs.

Next day, Christmas Eve, Rupert and his pals are snowballing on the common when they hear the sound of an airplane. Everyone looks up. It is the cowboy's machine with the Professor's servant in the back. He waves to Rupert. "What's all that about?" his chums ask. "Do tell us all." "Well," says Rupert as his pals gather round, "it's really the happy ending to a long story about some very curious fruit, an island and one of the Professor's inventions." The End.

RUPERT

*"Who is that new boy over there
All by himself?" asks Rupert Bear.*

Rupert is nearly late for school. Dr. Chimp is calling everyone in as he hurries into the playground. By the wall he sees a strange boy. "Who's he?" he asks Bill Badger as they file into class. "Don't know," Bill says. "He just stood by himself." Then Dr. Chimp comes in with the boy, a not very friendly looking lad in a kilt. "This is the Squire's grandson Hamish who comes from Scotland," Dr. Chimp says.

and HAMISH

"Hamish is Scots. He's here to stay
With Squire – a sort of holiday."

"To make friends, Bill I thought I'd try.
But he ran off. Perhaps he's shy."

Hamish, it seems, is visiting his grandfather and is to attend the school while he is here. He doesn't look pleased about it, neither smiling nor talking. "Probably shy," Rupert tells Bill. "Let's make friends after school." But after school Hamish hurries away. The pals go after him and catch up by the river. "Would you like to play," Rupert begins. "No," the boy says in a cold voice and turns away.

"Hey, Hamish, would you like to play?"
"No!" snaps the boy and turns away.

John Harrold.

RUPERT TRIES TO MAKE FRIENDS

*"He can't have meant to sound so rude.
I'm sure he just misunderstood."*

*"Let's look for him tomorrow then,
And try to make friends once again."*

*They look all over, then he's spied
Loitering by the riverside.*

*"We need one more to play and thought
Of you." He says he'd rather not.*

Bill is having tea with Rupert and as they eat they tell Mrs. Bear about Hamish. "He really is awfully rude," Bill says. "He didn't talk to anyone at school and when Rupert and I tried to make friends he walked away." "Oh, dear," Mrs. Bear says, "you must have misunderstood each other. Do try again. Make him feel you need him." The pals agree and as Bill leaves, Rupert calls, "Let's invite him to join a game of football with us all tomorrow."

Next day Rupert and Bill tell their pals about their plan. "I'm sure he'll join in if we say we really need him to make up sides," Rupert explains. Edward Trunk, Algy and Bingo aren't so sure, but agree when Rupert says that Hamish is probably just shy. So off they go in search of him and once more find him by the river, loitering. "We need someone to make up sides for football," Rupert greets him. "No thanks," Hamish grunts and turns away.

RUPERT THINKS OF A PLAN

"I'm sure he's lonely. Do try, dear,
To make him feel he's needed here."

Then later as he lies in bed,
A plan comes into Rupert's head.

For Rupert's plan they need a raft,
And this old door will be their craft.

He haunts the river so, this boy.
They plan to use it for their ploy.

"Well, did you try to make Hamish feel he's needed?" Mrs. Bear asks Rupert at bedtime. He sighs: "We did try." And he goes on to tell how they found him and told him he was needed to make up sides for football. "But he refused – and rudely," Rupert winds up. "He seems to want only to loaf about by the river." "Be a dear and try once more," pleads Mrs. Bear. "I'm sure he's lonely." Of course, Rupert agrees, and later in bed he thinks of a plan.

"Your idea better work after all this," Bill pants as Rupert and he carry an old door from his garden shed next day. "Sure to," Rupert says. "Since Hamish seems so fond of the river we'll use it. If he thinks we're in danger, drifting away on a raft, he'll rescue us and we'll have shown him he's needed. This door's our raft." So a little later the pals are hiding by the river waiting for Hamish. "Here he comes," whispers Rupert. "Get ready to launch!"

RUPERT'S PLAN GOES WRONG

"We'll make him think that we're afraid,
Adrift, and badly need his aid."

Their cries make Hamish start and stare
As if dismayed to see them there.

But what's this? They're gathering speed!
Now someone's help they really need!

Then down the towpath Hamish flies.
"I'll get you at the bridge!" he cries.

When Rupert thinks Hamish is near enough he whispers, "Into the water with it, Bill!" They push the door-raft clear of the bank and jump on board. The raft drifts to the middle of the river. Hamish is now quite close but he seems sunk in thought. Bill nods to Rupert. "Help!" they yell. "We're adrift! Save us!" Startled, Hamish looks up. But he doesn't rush to the rescue as Rupert expected. Instead he stares as if dismayed to see anyone there!

The pals try again. Sounding really quite frightened, they cry, "Please help us, please!" Then something happens that really does scare them. The raft begins to gather speed, cutting faster and faster through the water like a motorboat. But now Hamish springs into action. "Hang on!" he yells and races along the bank after them. "I'm going to try to stop you at the bridge." But hard as he runs, the raft seems to be drawing away from him.

RUPERT IS BAFFLED

But Hamish gets there just too late.
The raft has moved at such a rate.

"Shooglie!" the pals hear Hamish call.
They stop so hard they nearly fall.

More strange words are by Hamish cried.
The raft moves gently to the side.

"I can't explain this now, I fear.
But after supper meet me here."

"Oh, what's happening?" Bill wails as Rupert and he try hard not to fall off the speeding raft. They can see Hamish racing along the bank but the bridge is looming over them and Hamish has hardly reached it. The raft sweeps under the bridge and is quite a way downstream when Hamish appears on the the bridge. He shouts something. It sounds like "Shooglie!" And to the utter amazement of the pals the raft stops at once almost throwing them off.

Then from the bridge Hamish shouts again. But the pals can't understand the words. To their astonishment the raft moves gently to the bank where Hamish runs to help them off. "How did you do that?" Rupert gasps. Hamish shakes his head. But the pals keep on at him until he says, "Look, I can't tell you now. But, if you can keep a secret, meet me here after supper tonight and I shall explain then, right?" The very puzzled pals agree.

RUPERT MEETS SHOOGLIE

Hamish has brought a bucket when
He meets up with the pals again.

He calls out and before their eyes
The strangest creature starts to rise.

"We're such good friends at home that he
Has followed me down here by sea."

"His name is Shooglie and he dotes
On plain old-fashioned porridge oats."

After supper Rupert and Bill make their way to the riverside as arranged. Hamish arrives just after them carrying a big wooden bucket. "What's that for?" Bill asks. "You'll see in a moment," Hamish says mysteriously. "But first you must promise to keep secret anything I tell you and anything you see." The pals promise. Hamish turns to the river. "Shooglie!" he calls. For a moment nothing stirs in the dark water then Rupert and Bill cry out at what they see.

No wonder! For from the river rises a huge creature. Balanced on its back is the door-raft. "This is my good friend Shooglie, the Loch Shoogle monster," Hamish announces. Shooglie smiles. Hamish goes on: "When your raft took off today I guessed it had got stuck on Shooglie's spikes. So I stopped him and told him in our old Scots language not to show himself." Now Hamish holds up the big wooden bucket. "Here's your supper, Shooglie," he smiles. "Oats!"

RUPERT IS TAKEN BY SURPRISE

*"I tried to hide him. 'Twas hard luck
That on his spikes your raft got stuck."*

*Hamish is saying, "Now you see . . ."
A beam of light falls on the three.*

*It's P.C. Growler and it's clear
He doesn't know that Shooglie's here.*

*Then he looks up! "What's that?" he cries.
"Hamish's friend," Rupert replies.*

While Shooglie tucks into his supper and the pals lift the raft from his back, Hamish explains: "Shooglie was a baby when I found him near Loch Shoogle where I live. He was lost. So I took care of him in secret and we became great chums. When I came to visit Grandpa here Shooglie decided to follow by sea and river. I didn't think people would understand about him. . ."

"And that's why you kept near the river!" Rupert cries. Just then a bright light falls on the three and a voice says, "What are you lot up to so late?" It's P.C. Growler! What's more, it's plain he has not noticed the creature in the river behind. All three start to talk at once. "One at a time," Growler is saying when he looks up. "W-what's that?" he gasps in horror. "It's a friend of ours – or rather, of Hamish," Rupert says. "His name's Shooglie and he comes from Scotland." Shooglie lowers his great head and smiles into Growler's horrified face.

Rupert and Hamish

RUPERT SAVES THE POLICEMAN

*"Your grandfather the Squire shall hear
About this business, have no fear."*

*Next moment Growler's hanging by
His belt from Shooglie's jaws up high.*

*"Oh, do make Shooglie let him go!
It only makes things worse, you know."*

*"That monster creature and you three
Had better come along with me."*

As soon as the policeman has got over his shock he addresses Hamish: "Did you bring this here?" "In a way I suppose I did," Hamish says. "And does your grandfather know about this?" Growler goes on sternly. "Well, not really," Hamish admits. "Thought so!" Growler says. "I think you'll all come with me." He puts a hand on Hamish's shoulder and – whoops! – next moment he is hanging by his belt from Shooglie's jaws. And Shooglie isn't smiling now.

"Make it put me down!" Growler cries. But Hamish folds his arms and declares, "Shooglie does not like to see people lay hands on me." "I didn't lay hands on you!" protests Growler. "I only touched you on the shoulder." "Please tell Shooglie to put him down," Rupert pleads. "It will only make things worse if you don't." Grudgingly Hamish agrees and next minute the three youngsters and Shooglie are being led off to Nutwood's police station.

RUPERT GOES WITH GROWLER

He's much too big to go inside
So to a clothes pole Shooglie's tied.

"The Squire is still not home you say?
Well, we can have the lad to stay."

"Too far to take you home tonight.
So you stay here. You'll be all right."

As off they go they don't see that
A hot coal's landed on the mat.

At the police station which is also Growler's home Shooglie is left outside. Rupert and the others are led indoors. The policeman tells Bill and Rupert, "I'll take you two home after I've 'phoned the Squire and asked him to collect his grandson." But when he telephones he learns that the Squire has had to go to the city and won't be back until late. He has taken the car so his housekeeper can't fetch Hamish. Mrs. Growler who has come to see what's up, speaks: "Hamish can share our children's room tonight."

So that takes care of Hamish for the night. As kind Mrs. Growler ushers him upstairs her husband tells him, "Your grandfather will come for you in the morning and we'll see then what he thinks of you bringing nasty monsters to our nice quiet village." Then he turns to Rupert and Bill. "Now I'll take you home." He leads them out but as they go something happens that no one sees. A hot coal jumps from the living room fire onto the hearth rug.

RUPERT SPOTS A BLAZE

"Oh, P.C. Growler, see that glare!
A house must be on fire back there!"

"It's my house!" Growler gives a shout.
"Let's pray they've all got safely out."

The whole downstairs is blazing when
They reach the Growler home again.

Then round the back they dash – and stare!
The "monster fire escape" is there!

As P.C. Growler takes Bill and Rupert to their homes he grumbles about "youngsters who ought to be safe in bed, not larking about with nasty great monsters". Then something makes Rupert turn round. "Look!" he cries. "Something's on fire!" The others swing round to see a glow in the sky. "It must be a house," Bill says. "It's mine!" cries Growler. "Quick! Back to the police station. My family are there and so's your friend." The three start to run.

When they reach the police station they are stopped in their tracks by what they see. The ground floor is blazing fiercely. "My family and the lad!" Growler cries. "Trapped upstairs!" The three dash to the back of the building to see if there's any way in there. What a scene greets them! Shooglie has stretched his neck up to the window like a fire escape and Mrs. Growler is sliding to safety down it. The others are safe on the ground.

RUPERT SEES SHOOGLIE RETURN

Then off darts Shooglie through the gate.
"No, no!" cries Growler. "Do please wait!"

"The Fire Brigade's too far from here.
The whole place will burn down, I fear!"

"It's Shooglie coming back! I say,
He's coming from the river way."

He puckers up his lips and blows
As well as any fireman's hose!

"Clever creature!" Growler exclaims. "Not a nasty great monster, after all!" laughs Rupert. Then without warning Shooglie races off through the police station gate. "Come back!" Growler yells. "You're not going to get into trouble!" But Shooglie has vanished into the darkness towards the river and Growler is too concerned about the fire to follow him. "We'll never get this out on our own," he groans. "And the Fire Brigade couldn't get from Nutchester in time."

Rupert, who can't believe that Shooglie who has been so brave and clever would run away, wanders out into the road and looks towards the river. Suddenly he hears something heavy moving fast and out of the darkness bounds Shooglie. The monster dashes up to the building, points his head at the flames, puckers his lips and blows a jet of river water into the heart of the fire putting it out at once. Growler shakes his head in amazement – and admiration.

RUPERT MAKES A JOKE

*Says Growler, "I'm ashamed to say
I thought that you had run away."*

*"The Growlers must stay with me then
Until their house is fit again."*

*Soon Hamish must be leaving so
Shooglie decides that he will go.*

*"If only Shooglie could have stayed
He might have been our Fire Brigade!"*

Shooglie is a hero. P.C. Growler pats his head and says, "To think I imagined you'd run away when all the time you'd gone to get water. I am truly sorry." Just then there turns up the Old Professor who has seen the fire from his tower and come to see if he can be of help. When he hears all that has happened he says, "The Growlers must stay with me until their home is repaired. And Shooglie shall have the use of my private lake until he goes home."

At last it gets near the day for Hamish to go home. Shooglie decides to leave first to be there to greet him. His new friends, including the Squire, come to say goodbye. "On behalf of everyone in Nutwood I thank you, Shooglie," the Squire declares. Shooglie smiles at everyone then starts down the river towards the sea. As he watches him go Rupert chuckles: "It's a pity he can't stay. Think what a splendid village fire engine he'd make." The End.

Your Own Rupert Story

Title:_____

Why not try colouring the pictures below and writing a story to fit them? Write your story in four parts, one for each picture, saying what it shows. Then, faintly in pencil, print each part neatly on the lines under its picture. When they fit, go over the printing with a ball-pen. There is space at the top for a title.

RUPERT and

Rupert is glad to see one day
His friend Sam who has been away.

Sailor Sam is an old friend so Rupert is delighted to see him home from a trip. Sam, it seems, has been to the coast to see an old shipmate, Tom Tupper, who wrote to say he had something important to tell Sam. "But the poor old chap couldn't remember what it was when I saw him," sighs Sam. "His memory's awful . . . hey!" He breaks off and points to his cabin. "I left that window shut tight," he whispers.

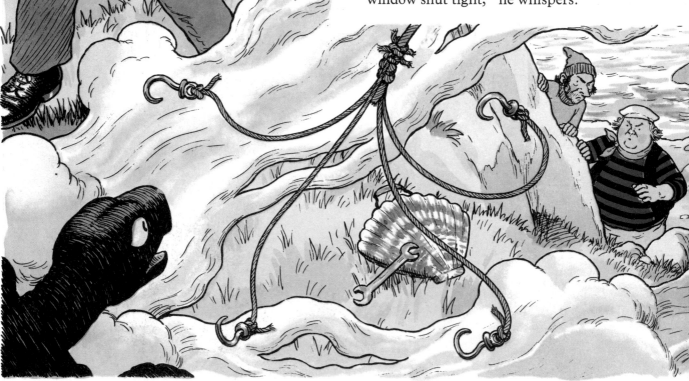

OLD TOM'S TROVE

"Hey," Sam says. "Something isn't right.
I left that window there shut tight."

"It may quite well have been a crook
Who broke in here. I'll take a look."

"Why are you whispering?" Rupert asks. Sam
puts a finger to his lips: "'Cos it's plain someone's
broken in and they may still be inside," he
breathes. "Wait here and I'll take a look." So
while Rupert watches nervously, Sam steals to
the door and lets himself in. Silence. Then a
cry. Sounds of a scuffle. And through the open
window flies, of all things, a model sailing ship to
land near Rupert!

From inside comes an angry shout.
And then a model ship's thrown out.

RUPERT MEETS A THIEF

The ship is followed by the crook,
A fellow with a weasely look.

He doesn't stop when with a roar
Sam comes a-hurtling through the door.

"I know you well, Eel Grubs!" Sam cries
As off in hot pursuit he flies.

But minutes later Sam is back.
His ankle took a nasty whack.

Without thinking, Rupert starts towards the model ship. He is reaching for it when a figure scrambles onto the sill of the open window and jumps out. He is a thin man with a nasty weasely face. He looks thoroughly scared. He stares at Rupert, then at the model ship. He makes as if to snatch it up. But at that moment there is an angry roar from the cabin and the sound of Sam making for the door. "Drat!" snarls the man. He turns and bolts as fast as he can move just as Sam bursts out of the cabin. Sam races after him, but in a few minutes he comes limping back. "Banged my ankle in that scuffle. Couldn't run fast enough," he pants. "But I recognised him. Nasty piece of work, name of Elias Grubs. Other sailors call him Eel on account of his being such a slippery customer. Been both pirate and smuggler in his time." "I'm afraid he's damaged your model ship," Rupert says. Then he adds, "It seems an odd thing to want to steal."

RUPERT MAKES A DISCOVERY

"'Twas Old Tom I've just been to see.
Who left that model ship with me."

"This hatch thing has come loose, I fear.
But wait! There's something inside here."

The finds look far from exciting,
A knotted cord, some old writing.

Sam's sure the writing is a clue
And thinks the knotted cord is too.

While Sam makes tea for the two of them he says, "You're right. It is an odd thing for someone like him to steal. It's not even a very good one. Come to think of it, it was Old Tom Tupper I've just been to see, who asked me to look after it afore he went on his last voyage . . . I say, what's up?" Rupert has given a gasp of surprise: "It's this hatch on the model. It's been shaken loose. It comes off. And there's something inside!" "Can you see what it is?" asks Sam.

"Not really," Rupert says. "But wait a moment . . . I can just get my hand in . . . I say, this is exciting." But what he pulls out isn't at all exciting looking. A knotted length of cord and a grubby bit of paper with writing on it. While Sam studies the cord Rupert reads aloud: "If in its name 'twere 'U' not 'O' to feed a Lord Mayor it might go." He looks up: "A riddle, Sam?" "No, I think it's a clue," Sam replies. "So is this cord!"

RUPERT JOINS SAM'S SEARCH

*"These knots are writing Indian style
Which tell us where to find an isle."*

*"Aye, Dolphin Isle of pirate fame.
'Tis treasure sure. That's Grubs's game."*

*"For Dolphin Isle we'll sail today!
Go ask your parents if you may."*

*Says Mr. Bear, "I say he should.
The sea trip's bound to do him good."*

"The knots on the cord tell us a position on a map," Sam says. "Each group is a number. Together they tell where to look. Old Tom learned this way of remembering things from the Indians in South America." He writes down the numbers then gets out one of his charts and studies it. "Here it is," he says. "Dolphin Isle." "But why all the secrecy?" asks Rupert. "For the same reason Eel Grubs tried to get the model," Sam says. "Treasure, I'll wager! This must have been what Old Tom wanted to tell me. He must have been meaning me to go after it – and I shall, right away! And I'd be pleased for you to join me." So not many minutes later Rupert is pleading with his parents to let him go and Mr. Bear is saying to Rupert's Mummy, "I think we should say yes. We know Sam will look after him. What's more the sea trip will do him good." So Rupert's bag is packed and off he hurries to join Sam.

RUPERT GIVES THE GAME AWAY

As for the coast our two set out
They're followed by a man who's stout.

And at the port he's there again,
The same fat fellow from the train.

Cries Rupert, "To Dolphin Isle, ho!"
Says Sam, "Don't let the whole world know."

It comes too late, Sam's warning word.
The fat man and his mate have heard.

The first stage of the journey to Dolphin Isle is a train trip to the coast. Rupert and Sam are so excited that neither notices a man who has been watching them from behind a pile of luggage and who jumps aboard the train as it is pulling out. The man is still lurking behind them as they leave the station at the seaport and make their way to Sam's boat, the Venture. "Fine craft," Sam says. "Engine and sails. I bought her from Tom when he left the sea."

Soon the Venture is ready for sea. As they head out of port it is such a perfect day for the start of an adventure that Rupert can't help calling out excitedly, "To Dolphin Isle, ho!" "Hush!" warns Sam. "Don't let the whole world know. You can't be too careful on this sort of trip. Still, I don't think anyone heard." He's wrong. The man from the train heard. His name is Fat Fred. And so did the man skulking behind some barrels with him – Eel Grubs!

RUPERT TRIES TO SOLVE A CLUE

"This riddle about 'O' and 'U',
I'm sure that it's the treasure clue."

"If in its name 'twere 'U' not 'O'
To feed a Lord Mayor it might go."

"Land ho!" brings Rupert from his bed.
And there lies Dolphin Isle ahead.

To find the treasure hereabout
They've first to work the riddle out.

The Venture is old but she's fast. "We should reach Dolphin Isle early tomorrow," Sam says. "Meanwhile we must start work on that riddle, I'm sure it tells where the treasure is to be found." So they read it over and over again: "If in its name 'twere 'U' not 'O' to feed a Lord Mayor it might go." But, try as they will, they are none the wiser by the time Rupert goes to bed and he falls asleep in his bunk murmuring the mysterious words of the riddle.

"Land ho!" The cry brings Rupert scrambling out into the open where Sam is still fresh and smiling despite having steered all night. And there is Dolphin Isle! As the Venture noses in to the shore Rupert says, "About the riddle – I thought hard about Lord Mayors but all I could think of was Dick Whittington of London." "Me too," Sam says. "And I can't see what he has to do with 'U' or 'O' and feeding Lord Mayors. But here we are. Let's get ashore."

RUPERT MEETS A TORTLE

Rupert decides he'd rather keep
His feet dry so he tries a leap.

"Turtles!" Sam cries. "They are the beasts
Once used for soup at Lord Mayors' feasts!"

"The clue suggests an 'O' not 'U'.
A 'tortle'? That will never do."

"There are such things as tortles. See!
You're looking at one now. It's me!"

When the Venture is anchored Sam and Rupert start ashore. Sam wades but Rupert prefers to keep his feet dry. He decides to jump on to what looks like a rounded rock in the shallows and from there to the beach. He measures his distance – jumps – lands on the "rock" and is pitched, limbs flailing, onto the sand. The 'rock' raises an angry head and as Rupert picks himself up he hears Sam cry, "That's it. The answer to the riddle – turtle. Turtle soup! It's what they have – or used to have – at the Lord Mayor of London's banquet each year!" Rupert repeats the riddle to himself: "If in its name 'twere 'U' not 'O' . . ." Aloud he says, "But that would be tortle. It makes no sense. There's no such thing." "You're looking at one," croaks a new voice. And the creature Rupert mistook for a rock emerges from the water. But it does not have the sort of flippers turtles have. It has feet like a tortoise!

RUPERT HEARS OF THE HERMIT

"The Hermit is a tortle too.
He'll be the one who's sought by you."

"Alone he lives in the next bay."
So there the two friends make their way.

"The bay looks empty, little bear.
No sign of any Hermit there."

A sudden screech, "Gobaack! Gobaack!"
A parrot dives in to attack.

"We're sea-going tortoises," the tortle says. "Very rare. The Hermit – the one you seek – is a tortle too." "What do you mean?" demands Sam suspiciously. "The Hermit is the only reason you'd come here," says the tortle. "He's known as the Hermit because he lives alone – in the next bay. He doesn't like others to see him as he is." "The next bay?" Sam repeats. "Come on, Rupert let's have a look." A moment later the two are striding along the beach.

As they scramble up the headland between the bays Rupert asks, "Why do you think the Hermit wants no one to see him?" "We'll find that out when we find the Hermit," pants Sam. They climb the last few feet and look down into a small sandy bay. Their eyes sweep it from end to end. "Not a sign of anything," Sam says. Suddenly the silence is shattered. "Gobaack! Gobaack!" Screeching angrily a brightly coloured parrot dives on Sam and Rupert.

RUPERT'S FRIEND FINDS A CAVE

Sam's shouting drives the bird away
Towards the far end of the bay.

"Come on!" Sam cries. "It's shown us where
The Hermit tortle has its lair."

As Rupert tracks the parrot's flight
He thinks, "I'm sure that Sam is right."

Here in the rocks they end their chase.
A cave! The Hermit's hiding place?

"Get off! Stupid bird!" Sam yells and waves his arms. Screeching, the parrot swoops across the bay. Rupert keeps his eyes on it until it vanishes behind some rocks. "Sam," he says, "I think that parrot was trying to stop us getting to the Hermit . . ." Sam turns to Rupert, his face breaking into a grin and finishes for him, ". . . and he's just flown straight towards where his friend the Hermit is hiding! Come on!" He dashes down to the beach with Rupert following.

"Silly bird!" Rupert thinks hurrying after Sam. "It draws attention to itself then goes right to where I'm sure the Hermit is hiding." As Sam and he get near the spot where the parrot vanished it pops from behind a rock as if to check that it isn't being followed, sees the two, squawks and disappears again. Sam stops when he gets to the rocks and waits for Rupert. "Look," he breathes. "It's in there, I'm sure." "A cave!" Rupert gasps.

87

RUPERT SEES THE HERMIT

Out from the cave the parrot flies.
"Gobaack! Gobaack! Not here!" it cries.

"I'm sure the Hermit's here," says Sam.
A weary voice croaks, "Here I am."

Then slowly plods into the light
The strangest, truly dazzling sight.

The Hermit looks so tired and old
Beneath a "shell" of gems and gold.

Rupert and Sam steal towards the cave. Suddenly . . . "Gobaack! Gobaack! Not here!" The parrot bursts from the shadows screeching and fluttering wildly. "We're not stupid!" Sam tells it scornfully. "You wouldn't make this row if there was nothing here!" But the parrot goes on squawking and fluttering. Then another voice is heard. A weary voice. "You're right. But Poll does mean well." And something begins to lumber out of the darkness inside the cave.

Rupert and Sam hold their breath as they peer into the gloom at the shape moving towards them. Then their eyes widen and Rupert gives a little gasp. A large, very old looking tortle emerges. But such a tortle! Rupert and Sam have to shield their eyes when the light strikes it. Its own shell is completely hidden by one made of gold studded with glittering gems. The friends stare in silence for a moment then as one they exclaim, "Oh, you poor thing!"

RUPERT DECIDES TO HELP

*"A Sea Gnome goldsmith Blackheart caught
Was forced to load me with this lot."*

*"It was that pirate's cruel jest
I was his living treasure chest."*

*"On Anvil Isle across this sea
Live Sea Gnomes who could set me free."*

*The Hermit weighs too much to swim.
Our two say they'll fetch help for him.*

"Who did that to you?" Sam asks gently. The Hermit sighs: "A Sea Gnome, one of King Neptune's goldsmiths. But he had to be forced to do it by Blackheart the pirate who'd captured him. That pirate called me his living treasure chest. Then he marooned me here with Poll his parrot because Poll befriended me and the Sea Gnome." "How did he know you'd stay here?" Rupert asks. The Hermit sighs again: "Because the treasure-shell makes me too heavy to swim. If I could swim I'd go over to Anvil Isle." The Hermit nods towards the horizon. "I'd ask the Sea Gnomes who work there to take it off." "Couldn't some other sea-creature fetch help for you?" Rupert asks. The Hermit says, "They're scared of what Blackheart would do if he found out. I can't blame them." Rupert thinks for a moment. "Then we shall go to Anvil Isle and fetch help," he declares. "Come on, Sam!" As they leave the Hermit calls, "Poll will come and guide you."

89

RUPERT GETS A NASTY SHOCK

But when they get back to the boat
No longer is their craft afloat.

"Eel Grubs," Sam says. "That man I chased.
"I'll wager that our trail he's traced."

The tortle says, "There came two men
Who sank your boat then left again."

"I heard a bit of what they said.
One was called Eel and one Fat Fred."

But when Sam and Rupert reach the place where they left the Venture a terrible sight greets them. All that is to be seen of their craft is the mast and the point of the bows. "What . . . how?" gasps Rupert. "Scuppered!" growls Sam. "Deliberately sunk!" "But who'd do that?" cries Rupert. Sam speaks quietly: "Remember Eel Grubs who tried to steal the model ship? It's just the sort of thing he'd do if he'd followed us. I'll wager he's found his way here!"

As he watches Sam wade out to the Venture to see if anything can be saved, Rupert remembers with a guilty start how he shouted the name of their destination as they left port. Suddenly – "Eel!" comes a loud croak that makes Sam turn back. It's the first tortle. "One of the two men who came in a boat and sank yours was named Eel," it says. "I heard them talking. Tortles can hear quite well underwater. They called each other Eel and Fat Fred."

90

RUPERT TAKES A TORTLE-RIDE

*"It's even more important now
We go for help. But tell me how!"*

*The tortle smiles, "If you forced me,
I'd have to take you 'cross the sea."*

*So Rupert starts his tortle-ride
With Poll the parrot as their guide.*

*The Sea Gnomes, Rupert learns from Poll,
Do not like visitors at all.*

"Where did they go?" Sam asks. "They said they were going to look for the treasure – I suppose they meant the Hermit," the tortle says. "Now it's even more urgent we get a Sea Gnome to free the Hermit!" Sam cries. "But how?" The tortle speaks up: "I'd go if it weren't for what Blackheart would do if he found out." A gleam comes to Rupert's eye and he says, "They couldn't blame you if I forced you to take me." "You've forced me," smiles the tortle.

So with Rupert pretending to be fierce and the tortle to be scared the two set out for Anvil Isle with Poll leading. "I'll guard the Hermit 'til you get back," Sam calls as Rupert shakes his seaweed reins and they head out to sea. The tortle moves at a surprising speed. "Have you ever been on Anvil Isle?" Rupert asks Poll. "Not actually on it," Poll says. "Being Neptune's goldsmiths the Sea Gnomes don't like strangers there."

RUPERT REACHES ANVIL ISLE

There's Anvil Isle, the Sea Gnomes' base.
A rocky, barren smoky place.

Those aren't volcanoes, Rupert's told,
But forges where they melt the gold.

The tortle stays close by the shore
While Rupert sets out to explore.

A hissing then a fiery roar,
And smoke clouds from the forges pour.

At last Anvil Isle appears. It is steep and bare and seems to be made up of lots of little volcanoes. On one side, joined to the island by a sort of bridge, rises a pillar of rock with an anvil-shaped top. The tortle lumbers ashore and Rupert dismounts. "Are those volcanoes?" he asks Poll. No, he is told. They are the forges where the Sea Gnomes melt and shape gold for the treasure chests of their master King Neptune in his underwater kingdom.

No one appears and the only sound is the swish of the sea. So, not feeling at all brave, Rupert says, "I suppose we'd better try to find someone." Poll settles nervously on his shoulder and they set off up a rough track. The tortle stays by the water. Suddenly as Rupert and Poll make their way between the forges there is a hissing then a fiery roaring. From the forges billow clouds of smoke which swirl around the pair, blotting out the sky.

RUPERT IS TAKEN CAPTIVE

Dense swirling smoke blots out the light,
And Rupert finds himself held tight.

"Oh, let me go!" poor Rupert yells.
Now he sees helmets shaped like shells

"No strangers here! A pirate spy!
Throw him into the sea!" they cry.

"To the Anvil!" and "Throw him back!"
They shout and march him up a track.

Rupert gasps as the smoke engulfs him. He can hear Poll squawking as it tries to fly clear of the smoke. Then he hears a patter of little feet a moment before he is grabbed and held tightly. "Let me go!" he pleads and struggles to get free. All he can see are dim shapes no bigger than himself. Then the smoke begins to disappear as if being drawn back into the forges and he can see that he is surrounded by helmets shaped like big sea-shells. As the last of the smoke clears he sees the helmets' wearers, plainly the Sea Gnomes, looking very cross indeed. Before he can speak the shouts go up, "Pirate spy! . . . No strangers here! . . . Away with him! . . . Back into the sea with the spy! . . . To the Anvil!" The next thing Rupert knows he is being bundled up a track. Then with a gasp of horror he sees where he is being taken – to the top of the anvil-shaped rock pillar, high above the sea.

RUPERT IS SAVED BY POLL

"'Tis Neptune's law that those who dare
Invade this isle are cast down there!"

A sudden shriek! The Sea Gnomes gape
At this furious feathered shape

The Gnomes are speechless, one and all
Then one cries, "Why, bless me, it's Poll!"

"I'm Zig. You made a friend of me
When Blackheart captured me at sea."

Rupert struggles and pleads, but in vain. At last the Sea Gnomes halt, and with a gulp he sees just how far above the sea he is. Now the Sea Gnomes fall silent. One of them addresses Rupert: "It is the law of King Neptune that any stranger who dares set foot on the island of his goldsmiths shall be cast back into the sea . . ." His words are drowned in a sudden wild screech and the startled Sea Gnomes let go of Rupert as a furious Poll dives on them.

Dumbfounded, the little creatures stare as Poll swoops and screams before settling on a rock just out of reach. "Good old Poll," Rupert thinks. "But how can a parrot help?" Then the silence is broken by a cry: "Why, it's Poll!" A smiling Sea Gnome goes up to Poll. "It's me, your friend Zig. I was rescued from Blackheart soon after you were marooned along with that poor tortle they forced me to turn into a living treasure-chest."

RUPERT PLEADS FOR HELP

"For helping me when I was low
Poor Poll here was marooned, you know."

"Rupert, my friend, is here to ask
If you'll perform a kindly task."

But then to Rupert's great dismay
The Gnomes refuse and turn away.

Except for Zig who says, "For you
I'll come and see what I can do."

Zig turns to the other Sea Gnomes and tells them how Poll, at the time Blackheart's parrot, befriended him when he was the pirate's captive and was marooned along with the Hermit for it. Then he asks Poll, "What brings you to our island, old friend?" Poll's answer is to fly down to Rupert's shoulder and say, "This is my friend Rupert Bear. He is not a spy. He has come to ask your help. Tell them, Rupert." So Rupert launches into his plea for one of the Sea Gnomes to come to Dolphin Isle and free the Hermit of his terrible treasure-shell. But to his dismay the Sea Gnomes turn away, shaking their heads. One of them says, "We never leave the island since Zig was taken prisoner on a journey." And looking rather shame-faced, the Sea Gnomes trudge away, ignoring Rupert's and Poll's appeals. All except Zig. "You helped me, Poll," he says. "And, anyway, I put all that stuff on the poor tortle, so I'll come."

RUPERT RETURNS WITH ZIG

*Into a craft by dolphins drawn
Zig loads his tools, collects his horn.*

*The shell-craft sets a cracking pace
As back to Dolphin Isle they race.*

*"Let's hurry," Sam says, "for I fear
Fat Fred and Eel are lurking near."*

*Says Zig, "Now, just leave this to me.
In no time we shall have you free."*

At Zig's words the other Sea Gnomes turn and stare. Then they cheer (for they really were ashamed at not being able to help). Suddenly all is bustle as a sea-chariot is got ready. This is a huge shell drawn by two dolphins. Zig puts his tool kit in the chariot and is handed a horn which he hangs over his shoulder. Now he joins Rupert in the sea-chariot. He flicks the reins to start the dolphins and soon they are racing over the sea followed by the tortle.

When at last the sea-chariot comes to a halt near the Hermit's cave Sam emerges. He is happy that Rupert has brought a Sea Gnome but he is worried too. While Poll is telling the Hermit the good news Sam confides, "I've got a feeling Eel and Fat Fred are nearby and spying on us." Rupert looks around and shudders. Then he takes Zig to meet the Hermit. "I'm truly sorry I had to burden you like that," Zig tells the Hermit. "But in no time I'll have you free of it."

RUPERT SEES THE HERMIT FREED

Says Sam, "I'll go and fetch some rope.
"There's some left in my boat, I hope."

"If that great load we're going to shift
I'll have to rig some sort of lift."

The Hermit gasps, "At last I'm free!
You can't think what it's like for me!"

Zig says, "All pirate loot must go
To Old King Neptune down below."

While Sam goes off to fetch rope from the Venture to lift the treasure-shell when it is undone, Zig sets to work. The Hermit stands with front and back feet on separate rocks so that Zig can wriggle underneath and undo the fixings. The Hermit which has always looked so sad really perks up. By the time Zig is done Sam is back with rope and hooks from the Venture's rigging. "Over here, please" he invites the Hermit as he slings the rope over a low-hanging palm tree. Four hooks hanging from rope are fixed by Rupert under the edge of the treasure-shell. "Haul away!" he calls to Sam on the other end of the rope. Sam heaves. Slowly the treasure-shell rises. Rupert has never heard such a sigh of relief as the Hermit's. Zig has unharnessed the dolphins and with Rupert's help moves the sea-chariot up to the treasure-shell. "In here, please," he asks Sam. "This must go to my master King Neptune."

RUPERT IS DISMAYED

*Zig's saying some reward there'll be
When there's a roaring out to sea.*

*Oh, no! The three friends stand aghast.
A motorboat is coming fast.*

*The three can only stand and look
As Fat Fred heaves a grappling hook.*

*Then with the treasure-shell in tow,
Scoffing and jeering off they go.*

With the treasure-shell in the sea-chariot, Rupert and the others take a break. The Hermit feels so light now and keeps sighing happily. Zig explains that all treasure won back from pirates must go to King Neptune who decides what happens to it. He is saying, "I am sure you will be rewarded in some way . . ." when his words are drowned by the roar of an engine. They swing round to see a motorboat racing at them. Eel Grubs and Fat Fred are in it!

Speechless, they watch the motorboat, roaring straight at the sea-chariot and the treasure-shell. Just when it seems it must crash into the sea-chariot Eel swings the motorboat round and slows to let Fat Fred hurl a grappling-iron. His aim is perfect. The hooks grip the edge of the sea-chariot and in the moment before Eel opens up his engine to tow away the treasure he jeers, "Thanks! We've been waiting for you to free this for us!"

RUPERT'S FRIEND SUMMONS HELP

A horn blast drowns the villains' jeers.
A mighty sea serpent appears.

Another blast. It grabs the shell
And drags it landward, boat as well.

A second serpent pops up when
The Sea Gnome sounds his horn again.

They grab the villains, swing them clear.
Cries Zig, "Your sentence you shall hear!"

With dismay Rupert watches the pair of rogues make off with the treasure-shell. After all he and the others have done! Suddenly Eel Grubs' cackling is drowned by a weird and wild sound. Zig has unslung his horn and is blowing it. Rupert gasps. For, in answer to the call, a great sea serpent raises its head from the sea. Another blast on the horn and the huge creature lunges at the sea-chariot and takes it in its jaws. Eel's jeering laughter gives way to squeals of fear and

Fat Fred is quaking with terror as the sea serpent pushes the sea-chariot shorewards and the motorboat with it. Then Zig sounds another blast. Up pops a second sea serpent. The two creatures dip their heads to the boat and each plucks a rogue into the air, squirming helplessly. Rupert and Sam laugh and Poll squawks with delight. "In King Neptune's name," Zig shouts at the pair, "I pronounce the punishment you must suffer!"

RUPERT AND SAM GO HOME

"You're banished to a distant isle.
And there you'll stay for quite a while."

"Since they sank your boat," Zig declares.
"It's only fair that you take theirs."

"I'm glad it's all worked out so well.
Now I'll take back the treasure-shell."

The Hermit, seeing off our pair,
Says, "Thank you Sam and Rupert Bear!"

"For trying to steal what is rightfully King Neptune's," Zig booms, "you shall be cast away on a distant island with very plain food and only water to drink for a very long time!" "Oh, not too long, please, Zig," Rupert whispers. "For a fairly long time," Zig corrects himself. Then as the whimpering villains are borne away he turns to Rupert and Sam. "You shall have their boat in exchange for the one of yours which the rascals sank," he declares.

Time to leave Dolphin Isle. Zig is returning to Anvil Isle. Poll and the Hermit are just going to enjoy being free. Rupert and Sam think it's time they headed home. So goodbyes are said and Dolphin Isle is left behind. The Hermit swims a little way with the motorboat. "It's wonderful to be able to swim again," it chuckles. "And it's thanks to two of the nicest people I have ever met. Goodbye and good luck, Sailor Sam and Rupert Bear!" THE END.